ELECTRIC

TREES

D1518457

Books by Melissa Bobe

ELECTRIC TREES
NASCENT WITCH
SIBYLS

ELECTRIC TREES

Gregg —
I hope you
enjoy the
journey...

STORIES BY MELISSA BOBE

Melissa Bobe

The Hive Press ⬣ New York

This is a work of fiction. All names, characters, organizations, events, and places are either products of the author's imagination or are used fictitiously. Any resemblance to actual places, events, or persons, living or dead, is purely coincidental.

ELECTRIC TREES

Previously published in *Alluvian*:
"Due North" (2018).

ISBN-13: 9798729375776

A Hive Press Book

Cover art & design by Melissa Bobe

*This book is dedicated to its readers,
in part to show my appreciation
but also because I want you to forgive me
for the journey I'm about to send you on.*

LIGHT

FISSURES

OUTAGES

LIGHT

Fins

It started in a bath, of course.

She laughed the first time, thinking how as a child, she'd stayed in baths until they ran icy cold and her mother was screaming from the kitchen for her to get the hell out already. She could still feel the chill of disappointment as she'd step shivering into the air, little fingers all pruned up, no scales or tail to be seen where her thin child's legs stood dripping beneath a scratchy towel.

But the edge of the gill wasn't on her leg; it was on her side, a little above her hip. That laugh had caught in her throat as she examined what was, after several moments, undeniable. After she'd dried herself off, it had seemed to fade. The following evening, though, the gill was there once more, joined by a twin on the opposite side of her torso, resting peacefully beneath the bath water. And she knew for certain then, although she was admitting nothing yet.

Two to start, then four, and then finally six slits, three on either side of her body, and she had to acknowledge that this would be the start of something she had hoped for as a child and never expected would visit her in womanhood, whether she was ready for it or not.

*   *   *

Every day on her way to and from work, she passed a lake house. It wasn't large, and she might never have noticed it except for the fact that it had a long, meandering path that led up to its front door, which was dark wood and seemed to reflect passing shadows and light like the surface of a lake itself.

The lake on which the house stood was not very large; it would have been considered more of a pond had it not been so deep. But the water was far from shallow, and the willows and other trees edging the surface seemed to shade it black, such that knowing what was below would be impossible without some applied source of light.

She hadn't gotten close enough to know all of this right away. She merely passed by each day as she walked to and from her job, until the evening came when she worked late and as such, caught a glimmer of light on her way home.

She approached hesitantly, feeling nosy and awkward, wondering why she should be so curious about a place that had nothing to do with her. She thought perhaps this was what it was like when you had a secret, a strangeness about you. By then, the gills that would appear in the bath were the least impressive change in her. The tail that had started to form each evening could be considered nothing less than majestic as it shone even in the dull light of the energy-saving bulbs above her bathroom sink. Even in her excitement, she had no one to tell, no one who could know this amazing new thing about her.

Perhaps people with secrets began to seek out the secrets of others, so that their own existence might feel less lonely.

The light was in motion, slow but almost bouncing, and as she drew close and passed by the side of the house, she caught its reflection and realized it was above the water. And then, she was close enough to see that its source was a lantern, held by an outstretched hand.

The old woman who walked on the surface of the lake stopped in her tracks, sensing an audience. She turned slowly, then nodded her head, the coils of white and grey hair not reflected in the water below, though they, too, shone in the lantern light. And the longer they gazed at one another, the less of a crone the woman looked; there was a lightness within that matched the brilliance she held in her hand, an ageless glow that came with a joyful knowledge about the self that one indulged in, protected and kept.

What could she say? She had stolen a secret; now, all that was left to do was for her to share her own. She slowly approached the lake, not yet ready for such deep waters as seemed to lie before her, and lifted her shirt over her head. Then she took two palmfuls of water and drenched her sides until gills flared open and the beginning of scales were shining in the glow of the lantern.

The old woman smiled. "Come back tomorrow," she said from the middle of the lake, then turned back around, content to stand vigil amidst the gentle waters lapping at her ankles.

*   *   *

She returned the next day as instructed. The old woman opened the door without her knocking, although it was early and she'd been wondering if she shouldn't have come after work instead of before.

"I've made tea," her hostess said, clearing away any worries that she'd arrived too soon.

They sat together in silence as the old woman carefully prepared two steaming cups. The cobalt blue of the glass mugs seemed a joke between them, though neither laughed aloud.

Finally, she decided that since she hadn't said a word yet, it was time to do so. "What are we?" she asked.

"Women, it would seem." A wry smile accompanied the response, and now the two of them did laugh together.

"You know what I meant."

The old woman tilted her head. "I do, but it's not the right question. We are not the same."

She nodded; that much was evident. Water gave her a tail, invited her to dwell within it. But it lifted the woman across from her up, denied her its depths and instead offered safe passage across its rippling surface.

"Okay," she amended, "why are we?"

"Why don't we begin with an introduction?" the old woman suggested. "That seems easier."

She nodded again, sipping at the tea to show that she didn't want to go first.

"I've taken to calling myself Yarelis."

The phrasing of this introduction wasn't lost on her, and she paused, not wanting to hear from this woman with whom she shared secrets the name that was used on her in the office, by clients, by ex-lovers, by people with whom she shared nothing at all.

"I'm Sirena," she said.

"Of course you are."

                    *   *   *

After a week of such visits, Yarelis offered Sirena a room in the lake house.

"I wouldn't want to impose," Sirena began, though her heart had given a hopeful jump at the idea of living in the beautiful house.

"This is a large place for one person to live. Besides, you have more questions than I can answer. The lake has offered me some explanations, exhaustive though they are not. It might help you understand the things you want to know, at least more than you do now."

Sirena said she'd think about it over the weekend and make a decision after that. What she did when she returned to her apartment was begin packing the few things she might care to take with her almost immediately. It didn't mean she was definitely going, she told herself. It just meant that if she did decide to accept Yarelis's offer, she'd be ready by the time the week started.

In the midst of her folding some clothing into a suitcase, the door to the apartment swung open.

"Hey, babe."

She said nothing, simply stopped in the middle of what she was doing to stare at him.

"What? You don't look happy to see me." As though he were entitled to the apartment with a lease on which he'd chosen not to put his name, Karl threw down his backpack and crossed his arms, frowning at her.

"You were gone for ten months," she told him, then went back to folding the shirt she had in her hands.

"So? I told you I was following the work." He walked over to her and looked down at the suitcase. "And where are you going?"

"How is that any of your business?"

"What's your problem?" he snapped, grabbing her by the arm.

This was why she'd hoped he'd gone for good. Shoving him off her, she thought with regret that she'd never changed the locks on the front door. "You don't live here, Karl—that's my problem."

"Oh, really?"

"Is your name on the lease?"

He glared at her. "You were always so fucking clingy. Suffocating and clingy."

"Yeah," she laughed bitterly, "wanting to know where my boyfriend is for months on end is super-clingy."

"I didn't come back here for this." He stalked over to the kitchen, threw open the refrigerator door, and started guzzling the orange juice she'd bought herself for the week.

Sirena started to argue, and then suddenly, a calming passivity took hold of her. There was no need for her to argue, the feeling said. She did not have to say anything at all. It wasn't giving in, she realized: it was letting go, and it pulled at her like a tide dragging away everything she didn't need, leaving only a desire for peace behind.

She looked into the suitcase. So far, she'd managed to pack a week's worth of clothes, a towel, two pairs of shoes, and a book of short stories that she'd always wanted to read but had never gotten around to starting.

It was more than she needed.

She threw her small purse into the suitcase, zipped it shut, then lifted it and made for the door.

"Where do you think you're going?" he demanded in her wake. "Hey, I'm still talking to you!"

She didn't turn around until she was several feet from the front door, in clear view of the adjacent apartments. "Don't worry," she told him. "There's another two weeks left on the place. You can stay until then."

"What are you talking about?" he hissed, not leaving the threshold of the front door as he glanced around.

She knew he'd be afraid to draw the attention of the neighbors, and she smiled. "After you were gone a few months and I'd heard nothing from you, I had my landlord change me over to a month-to-month lease. I don't have to pay anything beyond the next two weeks, and he can take the place back after that."

She left him there in the doorway, clenching his fists in a helpless rage. But really, the decision had been made for her. It wasn't like she could let Karl know her secret. It wasn't as though she wanted to.

The light from Yarelis's lantern guided her the final steps of the way. It was hanging on a small rod next to the front door, as though waiting for her arrival.

*   *   *

The days passed quietly at the lake house. In exchange for help cleaning and cooking, Yarelis granted Sirena a beautiful bedroom that overlooked the lake and as much good food as she wanted to eat. They didn't speak often, living side by side in a peaceful understanding that while they weren't the same, as Yarelis had said, they were kin of a kind, bound together by the waters that made each remarkable in her way.

The bathroom adjacent to the room where she slept had a huge, deep tub in which Sirena delighted. She would linger there for hours at a time, curled comfortably within the waters, her tail with plenty of room to unroll itself. There was not a moment that passed where she missed the old apartment, which had never felt like a home in the way this tub did.

Yarelis only entered the room once while Sirena was bathing. She smiled up at the older woman to demonstrate how happy she was.

"I'm glad you like it," Yarelis said, "though I wonder why you've never tried the lake."

And she hadn't, as of yet. There was something foreboding about the idea of allowing herself to be, to sit fully in her secret outside of a shut-away room, beyond an enclosed space with four solid walls and shut doors. She looked out over the black rippling waters from her windows every day, but she knew she wasn't ready to dive into them.

Without her saying anything, Yarelis seemed to understand. "I began in bathtubs, too," she told her in a gentler voice. "But don't stay in here forever, or I'll stop calling you Sirena and start calling you Melusine."

Although Sirena didn't understand, she dipped back beneath the water with a smile still on her face, gills widening and narrowing in a contented rhythm.

*   *   *

They continued discussions, often over tea, about who they were. Mostly, the conversations were Sirena's musings and Yarelis's insistence that she had no answers. What she did have, however, was a sprawling library on the ground floor of the lake house, directly beneath Sirena's room.

There, Yarelis had collected books on merfolk, sirens, selkies, naiads, and every other water-dwelling creature that was not supposed to exist. But now Sirena knew for sure that at least two of them did.

And while Yarelis offered no commitment to Sirena's hypotheses about how many others like them might exist, where they could be, and why they had come into being, she would sometimes reference these many works as a means of tidying her companion's more wild guesses.

"There's only one way to know for sure whether there are more to be found," she finally said one night.

"What's that?" Sirena asked, though deep down, she felt she knew.

"To swim into wider waters and see for oneself."

*   *   *

It was days before Sirena felt brave enough to consider what Yarelis had said. It was weeks before she drew up the courage to go forward into those waters. And in those weeks, her tail grew stronger and more majestic than ever, its scales glittering like gems beneath the still waters of the tub, a tub which, Sirena now realized, looked like more of a container that held her back than the instrument of joy she had once felt it to be.

Finally, the day arrived when she felt strong enough to tell her companion that it was time for her to step out of the house and into the lake it looked out over, to plunge into those black waters and see what lay beneath and beyond.

Yarelis smiled. "Tonight, then. I will go as far as I can with you."

It wouldn't be very far, Sirena knew, but she was glad that she would have company.

The night was not warm, and as they made their way outside, she considered turning back. Yarelis said softly, "You already know what's behind you."

Sirena continued forward, breathing through lips that were already beginning to turn blue.

Yarelis had brought her lantern, and though the cold air was upon them both, it offered a kind of warmth through radiance. Sirena turned her gaze towards it as she slipped out of the jeans and shirt she'd been wearing, then took steps into the high grass and reeds along the edge of the water.

Crickets sang happily, an owl hooted its presence from a nearby tree, and fireflies challenged Yarelis with intermittent brightness in the air above the lake. A thin crescent of a moon gleamed gently in the clear and cloudless sky. Sirena took a final breath of the night air, then dove forward.

The water of the lake was even colder than she'd expected, and immediately, she was glad that the change in her had produced more than just a tail. After repressing the chattering of her teeth for a moment, she found the urge to shiver left her as soon as her scales had come fully forward. Then, there was a soothing feeling of being home, of finding herself for the first time, of knowing she was where she ought to be.

She surfaced, found new gills above her collarbone, gleaming scales down both of her arms, and realized that her friend had been right: she had not allowed herself the fullness of her own existence in the tub. She looked up to see Yarelis smiling down at her, and, as she'd looked on that first evening out in back of the lake house, it was as though years had been lifted from her face as one foot and then the other extended out and onto the water, steps as easy and light as though she were walking across a stretch of carpet or moss on a low rolling hill.

The lantern light was bright and flickering, a joyful flame that partook of the bliss Sirena had found in these waters. They were brackish, she realized, and her fins told of a current that led out into a nearby river that would carry her towards the sea. She had a moment of fear, dreading the unknown, but then she realized: it was far worse to remain a shade of oneself than to risk swimming into new waters.

Her last glance up at Yarelis was through a clear second eyelid that promised she would not be swimming blindly forward. And Sirena realized that the lantern, with its reflected radiance bouncing on the gentle waves between them, was one of two sources of light in the water: the other came from her, from the bioluminescent glow of her own scales. She dove down into the black depths of the lake, her friend's lantern lighting the way until Sirena found the outlet into the river. Then all that was left to guide her was the light she carried as this, the truest iteration of herself.

Due North

Isabel couldn't understand what was so strange about wanting to go north to the polar bears. After she'd mentioned the idea to some of her friends, their reactions told her not to bring the subject up with anyone else. They regarded her as though she had gone crazy, like that man in the old documentary who was eaten by his pet grizzly bears. But who would want to visit a grizzly bear? And Isabel wasn't looking for pets; she was looking to make amends.

She thought that maybe she should bring a gift or something, though she wasn't sure what kind of a gift said: "Sorry for being part of the species that's melting the glaciers you live on. Sorry for adding to the heat that is starving your relatives and friends to death." How do you apologize for being human? It seemed there weren't words or gestures enough.

It was not difficult to go north. She'd had to read about proper attire and equipment, but thanks to the magic of shopping online, most of what she needed wasn't hard to get her hands on. The warm parka she'd purchased was a little disturbing, she had to admit. The color was louder than it had looked on the store website:

an unforgiving fire engine red that she'd rather not look at and certainly didn't want to wear. But it was the best coat available for the price, and this trip was not about fashion.

Isabel's savings weren't huge, but they were substantial; in the end, she had enough for gear, transportation and lodging, and the weeklong guided tour. Without another word to friends and family, she found herself on a plane overlooking tundra, near-blinded by the bleak, white glare from below.

She didn't talk much to the other travelers who made up the rest of the tour group, though a few tried to get to know her at first. She was patiently consistent in her silent smiles and drifting gaze, and eventually, they left her to herself. Over the course of the two days she had to wait for her planned bear encounter, she grew to detest the voice of the tour guide, who felt the constant need to remind them that, if they felt like they might be experiencing *too* much exposure to the cold, they must report it to him *immediately*. Isabel wondered how he managed not to spoon-feed everyone hot soup and tie their bootlaces for them, an impulse she was certain he struggled with.

On the third day, when the tour was finally going to venture further to see more wildlife, the tourists in Isabel's group were checking their camera bags obsessively to be sure they had enough spare batteries. She stared out at the landscape as the shuttle bus took them from their lodgings and further into snowy terrain, wondering with little interest what her fellow travelers hoped to capture with their expensive cameras. She heard the guide's grating voice remind them that they should not wander off on their own, that predator animals were *much* less likely to bother a large group of people and that their proximity to one another would *enhance* their experience as they marveled at nature's beauty *together*. She wished someone would open a window so that the snowfall swirling around the bus would blow in, fill his mouth, and shut him up.

It finally came time to park and go outside to search for whales, one of the creatures the tour had promised a glimpse of. The land seemed endless, a frozen desert that disappeared into itself on all sides, but after walking a few paces, Isabel found with burning eyes the edge of the arctic sea. The guide reminded them that they could only get so close to the water because they wanted to remain safe on solid ground, but if they were lucky, the whales would start spyhopping. A murmur of excitement rippled through the group like a shiver in the falling snow.

The whales were quick to come out of the water, to the delight of all the tourists. Taking advantage of the sounds of cameras, Isabel snuck away into the gust of a snowy wind. Once she knew her steps wouldn't make noise enough to distract the enthralled shutterbugs and their pontificating tour guide, she began to run from the group, past the shuttle and into the snow-covered beyond.

After a while, Isabel found that she was warm inside her parka from running, though her face ached in the unforgiving arctic wind. She stopped to look around. White upon white, no sign of the shuttle behind her. She knew she couldn't have outrun it by all that much in the short time she'd been traveling, but gone was the sound of coastal waters. She was left with the cold, the lonely singing of the wind her only companion in the otherwise completely silent world.

She shut her eyes: black. Opened them: white. Black, white, black, white, and she kept them closed, hoping for something that might not come. But just as she was about to open her eyes once more, she heard it: a slow-paced step, a shuffling gravity with breath that sounded far too thick to be human.

Isabel opened her eyes once more. Approaching her was a huge white bear. As their gazes met, he paused in his steps, then continued forward until he was standing before her. She reached out a hand, and the bear sniffed gently at her fingers.

She was overwhelmed by something that she didn't have the words to name, because she had never felt it before. Tears froze painfully to her face. "I'm sorry," she said aloud. Her voice wasn't hollow, as she had expected, but it was quiet. In that wide expanse of winter, there was nothing for her words to echo against. The snow seemed to muffle them so that only he could hear her. Isabel and the bear were alone in a world that offered its sole two occupants nothing but the privacy in which to share their deepest secrets.

He nuzzled her with his face, and she was amazed by how easy it was to hug him, just like you'd think it would be to hug a bear. He put a paw to her back and made a gentle huffing noise. They stood, holding one another for a moment that promised to be endless, until Isabel heard the sound of a distant horn and recognized what must be a searching shuttle bus looking for a vanished passenger.

She knew that, even off the road, her red parka might be visible against the otherwise white expanse. She unzipped it and threw it off, feeling an immediate jolt of cold push through her white sweater. She snuggled close to the bear. He made a little whine, and let her drape one arm over the massive base of his long neck. He took a step, slowly, waiting for her to walk with him before putting his huge paw down and moving his massive body forward. Together, they left the sound of the desperately honking horn behind, the last reminder of a world that did not belong to them.

Isabel didn't feel the cold standing next to the bear. She thought for a moment that she might have what the guide had called *exposure*, that there was no way she wasn't freezing to death in this wintery air. But walking came so easily, and she felt the bulk of the bear in her arms, saw him next to her, heard his chuffing, curious little breaths. She shed her fear like another coat and also left it behind.

The two walked together as night rose and day fell under the tundra before them, which hadn't yet disappeared into the encroaching ocean. They saw no water, only ice.

All of His Loved Ones

What Jonathan couldn't seem to communicate to the woman on the other end of the line was that having an elephant at a funeral, regardless of whether or not the ceremony was to occur outdoors, would be out of the question.

"But Mr. White, I don't think you quite understand the relationship between my cousins and the elephant."

"Ma'am, it's not a matter of understanding. This is just not—"

"I'm sure you'll appreciate the situation more once the girls speak to you in person. They should be there soon."

"They're coming here? Today?"

"Of course, Mr. White. My uncle had custody of the girls for most of their lives. They'll want to oversee all arrangements for his memorial."

It struck Jonathan that she'd mentioned custody. The old man had been eighty-six when he'd died, after all. How young could these "girls" possibly be?

"If you don't mind my asking, how old are your cousins?"

"Well, Sally's nineteen, and I believe Annabelle just turned eighteen."

Jonathan was unsettled by this new information, a feeling he didn't experience often. He thought of his own niece, who was sixteen years old, and how she might handle coming to a funeral parlor to make arrangements in the event of his brother's death.

"Ma'am, won't there be another relative with the two of them? You know, someone a bit...older? To help with the arrangements, I mean."

"Oh, no," she assured him. "That's not necessary. They're both very bright, and more than capable of going over everything with you. But I must insist you hear them out about the elephant, and that you ultimately allow it."

"Ms. Danton, again I apologize, but to have an elephant at our home—"

"I'm so sorry, but I really have to get going. I still need to call more of the family with the details so they can make their plans to attend the services. The girls will go over everything else with you. Thanks very much for your time."

"Ms. Danton, please. Will you just—Ms. Danton?"

Wonderful. Now Jonathan had to figure out how to tell two mourning teenagers that their pet elephant couldn't be present at their primary caregiver's funeral.

"Louise! Louise?"

He heard some shuffling going on upstairs, which meant his wife was cleaning something. It bothered him that she cleaned so much. The parlor was always spotless, as it should be—death was, if nothing else, a sanitary affair—but having their home upstairs in the same condition as the rooms below was irritating in a way he couldn't quite express to Louise. Jonathan felt that there should be some way of marking the difference between the life they led and the deaths they managed—some line drawn, some sign posted. With everything so damn clean, some nights he'd wake up to use the bathroom and wonder whether or not he was still alive.

He started up the stairs. "Louise!"

"What? Jonathan, don't come up here! I don't want your footprints messing up the hall!"

What footprints? He hadn't even left the house yet. "Louise, I have to talk to you."

She made a noise of exasperation, as though he was always interrupting her cleaning. Well, she was always cleaning, so perhaps he was. "What *is* it?"

"It's about the Danton service. They...they want to bring an elephant."

"They want to do what?"

"Bring an elephant."

"A *what*?" He tried to continue walking up the stairs, but she snapped, "You stay down there!"

"Louise! Will you just stop cleaning for a moment so I can—"

Three firm knocks sounded on the front door. Jonathan turned, thinking, *Who wouldn't try the bell first?* He made his way back down the stairs, crossed the front hall, and opened the door.

They weren't extraordinary-looking. Not that he'd necessarily expected them to be, though he hadn't really known what to expect of two girls who wanted to bring an elephant to a funeral. In fact, they were two of the more ordinary-looking people he'd encountered in his work, the type of mourners that usually sat in the second or third rows, blending in behind the immediate and more visibly bereaved family.

"Hello, I'm Jonathan White. You're—"

"Annabelle Danton, and this is Sally."

She had a stronger handshake than her elder sister, and there was something strangely direct about her. It wasn't that she'd interrupted him, though Jonathan hadn't expected that. Maybe it was the yellow sweater she wore. It was ugly, a dull mustard knit that hung sloppily about her torso. He wasn't sure anyone had ever entered the home wearing yellow. Louise preferred neutral tones; the brightest thing he'd ever seen her wear was periwinkle.

The older girl, Sally, was dressed more traditionally in black, but she didn't meet Jonathan's gaze. She was busy glancing around the front hall, to the extent that he wasn't even sure she'd noticed him at all, even after having shaken his hand.

Jonathan remembered himself, and replied, "Yes, of course. Please, come in."

They followed him to his office. Annabelle sat before he could gesture towards a chair. Her sister stood beside her, and, growing more flustered by the minute, he didn't know whether or not to offer her the other open chair. They both seemed inclined to do as they pleased (which was probably why they'd requested an elephant in the first place).

Jonathan resolved to say nothing to the elder girl, and sat behind his desk. "Now, Miss Danton, your cousin phoned me a little while ago. She said you were going to manage all of the arrangements—"

"We're here to discuss the elephant. And please, call me Annabelle."

"Well, Annabelle," Jonathan cleared his throat in an effort to disguise his unease, "as I tried telling your cousin earlier, we really don't have the...facilities for an elephant here."

She blinked at him for a long moment. Her face remained expressionless, but he sensed some strain in her, as though she were trying very hard not to mock him. "We've requested an outdoor service, Mr. White."

"Yes, of course, but...even so, I mean, you have to admit, it's a rather unusual...I mean...perhaps, are there photographs of your uncle and the elephant?"

Annabelle seemed to consider this. "No, I don't believe there are. Maybe. Why does that matter?"

"Well, we could produce a nice, enlarged print of a photograph of the two, and have that on display instead."

She shook her head once with resolve. "No, Mr. White. I'm afraid this is non-negotiable. We'll have the elephant present the day of the funeral, or we will have to make arrangements elsewhere."

That threw him. He hadn't expected a grieving adolescent would be so assertive. But he also hadn't expected that anyone would ever want to bring an elephant to the home, and that was fast becoming old news, apparently.

Jonathan wasn't entirely sure that he could afford to refuse such an ultimatum outright. At one time, he might have, but just the year before a new mortuary had opened up, and the competition was giving him and Louise trouble. They were a small family business, and while you might think people die every day, their town was only so big.

He thought of pointing out to Annabelle that her family was already making arrangements to come to the home and that it would be highly unlikely she might successfully move a funeral that was only a week away. But the thought nagged at him that he was no longer the only show in town, and furthermore, the girl seemed so resigned to the idea that he wasn't entirely sure she couldn't pull it off.

Just as he was about to say that he hoped they would not feel the need to switch homes—though he still couldn't agree to the elephant—the other sister, Sally, spoke up for the first time. "You have a very clean establishment, Mr. White," she told him in a soft, steady voice that was very different from Annabelle's. "I can see my sister's knees reflected in the wood of the front of your desk."

He waited for her to continue, but she simply turned her gaze from the desk up to him, her eyes inquisitive as though expecting him to respond. "Yes, thank you," he managed. "My wife keeps our home in very good order."

"I wonder," continued Sally airily, as though she had been on another planet for the duration of his conversation with Annabelle and had only just arrived to join them now, "I wonder if you have ever had a guest emit embarrassing bodily odors during a service."

"...I'm sorry?"

"I wonder," she repeated patiently, "if a guest at one of your services has ever smelled unpleasant due to bad personal hygiene." She paused, seemed to think for a moment, then added, "Or due to gas."

"Um...well, I suppose the odd guest has been a bit..." Jonathan felt his face reddening. "I'm sorry, Miss Danton—"

"Oh—Sally, please."

"Yes, of course—Sally, I—"

"And," she continued, "I wonder if there has ever been a family dog present at a funeral."

This gave him pause, as there had been a funeral just a month prior at which a pleasant-looking yellow lab sat beside one of the relatives of the deceased. He'd thought it unorthodox at the time that he'd been given no prior warning, but there was a good chance it had been a service animal, and he had decided it would likely be more trouble than it was worth to say anything.

He thought of lying to Sally about this incident, but for some reason felt it was better to be honest. "Yes," Jonathan admitted, "we have had a guest bring a dog—I believe, a *service* dog once before. But, if you think a dog and an elephant are comparable, I must—"

"I can assure you, Mr. White, that our elephant won't be emitting any foul odors or making anyone feel nearly as uncomfortable as past flatulent mourners likely have." She was looking at him with wide, sincere eyes as she made her promises. "Furthermore, as you've entertained animals before, it seems that you do have facilities for our elephant, after all."

He was stunned into silence. The girl was so even-tempered and poised, almost as though to convince him that any elephant accompanying her would doubtless be a beast with only the best manners. And, more astonishing, he felt he nearly *was* convinced of this, and only with great effort managed to continue arguing with her.

"I don't understand how you expect me to accommodate an elephant," he said weakly. "And frankly, I don't understand why the elephant must be present at all."

Annabelle and Sally looked at each other then, surprised. He wasn't sure what he'd said to cause such a response, but it gave him some small comfort to know he wasn't the only one who was going to be perpetually taken aback during the course of this conversation.

"Really?" asked Annabelle. "Our cousin didn't explain that on the phone?"

Jonathan shook his head, trying to steel himself for whatever rebuttal might follow.

"You have our apologies, Mr. White," said Sally, and she sounded truly apologetic. "That should have been the first thing she told you. We require that the elephant be present because we love it very dearly."

"That's all?"

The same quiet manner, the same patient tone. "Mr. White," she went on, "if the man who raised you had just died—a person you adored your whole life long and whose passing had just about broken your heart— wouldn't you require the company of all of those you loved as you bid him goodbye?"

*   *   *

The service was beautiful, as all who attended would later remark. The food was delicious yet tasteful, the wine sweet but just somber enough, and the flowers arranged so that they demonstrated both comfort and sympathy in equal parts. The day was warm, but fluffy clouds passed slowly overhead so that the sun never beat down on the mourners, and a gentle breeze kept suits and dark dresses from ever growing too warm.

Annabelle gave a lovely eulogy for her uncle as Sally stood by her side, and behind them both: the elephant. It wasn't as large as Jonathan had been anticipating; it was still an elephant, of course, but he'd imagined a great, looming beast that would trumpet and stamp about the grounds. Instead, the elephant stood quite peacefully, blinking its long-lashed eyes lethargically, shifting its weight every so often on its thick grey legs, and periodically nuzzling the girls' shoulders with its trunk. As Sally had promised, not once did it exhibit any flatulence, and, though he could smell it from where he sat behind the rows of mourners, it emitted an almost pleasant odor of warm hay. It was a smell that made death less clinical, he thought: familiar, unthreatening, and tranquil.

Louise sat beside him through the whole service, her eyes wide and her lips parted in amazement every time she took in the sight of the elephant. When she would intermittently glance over at Jonathan, she would remember to shoot him a fearsome look. He'd normally dread such an expression, but there was an elephant at his home and the world hadn't ended as he'd worried it might. He couldn't help but feel a great sense of relief as he looked upon his mammoth grey guest, standing by its family and minding its manners.

Later, Annabelle and Sally approached Jonathan to thank him for a wonderful service that they were certain their uncle would have appreciated. Sally remarked as an afterthought, "And perhaps this will help you attract more business."

"How's that?" he asked her, curious.

"Well, perhaps others who have lost someone and who would like to have *all* of their loved ones to comfort them will learn that you ensure such a thing is possible for your clients."

Had her sister spoken, he'd have thought she was mocking him again, but knowing Sally through the few interactions he'd had with her, Jonathan couldn't doubt her sincerity. He smiled and replied, "Well, I doubt we'll have any other requests about elephants."

"Really?" asked Sally. "Why would you doubt it? You've had our request already."

This struck a chord in him. The new mortuary was far too polished to accept such requests, surely. Any clientele interested in bringing elephants—or goats, or orangutans, or who knew what else—would have to come to his home instead. They would have plenty of business. And Louise would finally have a reason to clean.

He was broken from these thoughts by the sound of a car pulling away. The guests were all slowly filtering out, but he could find no trace of Sally, Annabelle, or the elephant. They had apparently taken their leave without another word.

The Rest of the Day Off

One day at the office, I read a story that made me stick a frowning-face sticker, perfectly round and neon green, on top of the stack of rejections growing on the corner of my desk.

Work is monotony. Paperwork comes through; you do with the paperwork the things that need to be done; you manage not to set the paperwork on fire in the process; in fact, you wisely choose to file the paperwork instead of taking a lighter to it (good for you, you get an extra cookie today for resisting pyromania); you finish the rest of the day's tasks; and you brace yourself for the paperwork that will come the next day.

The office across the way is a shiny new startup. Its employees not only have mixers and celebratory catering after the workday ends, but they are also allowed to bring their miniature schnauzers and French bulldogs and papillons with them to work, presumably to help them keep their sanity in an office that is fully stocked with alcohol and gourmet snacks at all times. I know about the dogs because I see them prance in with their owners at the start of business, and I know about the mixers and catered parties because when the workday ends for the startup folks, I'm still trying to wrap up the tasks that remain on my side of the hall.

I know what you're thinking, but the startup across the way is not hiring at the moment.

My coffee gets cold about thirty minutes into the day. This is because it comes with me from home, and don't think for one second I haven't tried every thermos, thermal mug, and insulated travel cup available. But the boss reminds us that having a coffeemaker in the office would require that an employee make coffee, and "you girls are just so fond of suing, we'll all have to play it safe and go without."

"You girls" have seen the boss drink a mild cup of tea and get the leg shakes. We know why there's no coffee to be had in the office.

Business as usual means days that stretch on, unless the one dachshund in the startup office has a meltdown. This has happened twice, and it is the thing I silently pray for every single morning on my train ride to work. The second time, he even made it into our office, and no one could catch him for a good twenty-five minutes. To be honest, when he ran past my desk, I only pretended to make a grab for him. In my mind, I was rooting for the little guy, especially when he pissed on a wholesale carton of caffeine-free tea in a corner of the office kitchen.

The day of the frowning-face sticker, I was keeping an eye out for the dachshund while reading the most recent issue of a literary journal I'd submitted to and been rejected from. This was lunch, which I typically took at my desk because if I went out, I might never come back.

One coworker was trying to hit on another uninterested coworker, which wouldn't have been anything to notice except it was the sixth consecutive workday on which he had made such an attempt, and I'd decided to start counting so I was obligated to pay at least a little attention to what went on around the office (aside from escaped dogs). I noted that around day four, he had started to demonstrate "Nice Guys of OKCupid" tendencies: getting politely turned down, smirking a little, wondering aloud if uninterested coworker had a boyfriend, remarking how it was amazing that whenever decent guys asked girls out they always seemed to have boyfriends, and other such bullshit.

I was beginning to hope the dachshund would piss on him next, but on this sixth day of creepy office let's-not-call-it-harassment-you-girls, I happened to be reading a fiction in which a male character is not invited into his date's home after their first dinner together. In the story, the protagonist, with whom readers are apparently meant to empathize, goes on to break into his date's home, rape and kill her, and then find his way into her computer so that he might look up his now-deceased date's younger sister and court her via a dating website. I finished the story and calmly rifled through my desk, seeking my sheet of assorted face stickers.

I was given the stickers by my last therapist just before I lost access to therapy due to the limits of my health insurance. As a parting gift, they've proven somewhat useful. I have difficulty expressing myself at times. A sticker can sometimes relate what you're not capable of saying:

I hate this job.

I hate men who harass women.

I hate men who write about impossibly charismatic men who kill women.

I would like to own a pissing dachshund but can't afford a dog-walker to cover working hours.

I'm not entirely sure there's a sticker to express that last thought. The therapist hadn't been great while the sessions lasted, so the stickers seemed like something of a win. The $18.95 I'd spent on the publication I was reading, however, was seeming like more of a waste with each second that my coworker spent bitterly discussing the incomprehensibility of women who did not want to date him.

I found my green sticker and determinedly pressed it down onto the rejection pile, which I kept at work to remind myself I had never really wanted this job in the first place. I shut my eyes and prayed for an earthquake.

To top everything off, the prose in that story had been mostly shit, too.

I didn't exactly feel myself get up. I knew it was happening, that it was drawing attention and that I must have had a strange expression on my face, but I couldn't even begin to care about how I looked. My rambling coworker trailed off, his most recent line about "frigid bitches" evaporating mid-sentence as I passed him by. I heard my boss say something about how "you girls think you can just come and go as you please," but he didn't quite finish his sentence, either.

What I do know is that I ended up on a train headed for the beach. It wasn't particularly warm out, but it wasn't winter yet, so there were other people on the beach-bound train. At one of the stops along the way, a person around my age sat down across from me and smiled. "I like your sticker," they said by way of introduction.

I tilted my head as though I were a neurotic pissing dachshund, confused by the compliment. Then I recalled that, at some point between my coworker remarking how no one was single when nice guys were asking and me leaving the office, I had grabbed another frowning sticker and smacked it on the front of my shirt, directly over my heart, pledging my allegiance to my own misery.

"Thanks." What else could I say? You have to appreciate someone who can appreciate a face sticker.

"Off from work today?"

"No, I just left."

"Do that often?"

I shook my head.

"I do," they replied.

"Is that what you're doing today?"

"No." Their eyes moved downward. "Today I left to visit my brother in the hospital. He'll be dead soon."

"Oh," I managed after a breath.

They shrugged. "Cancer."

I peeled the sticker from my shirt and offered it, hoping they wouldn't mind the mess of navy fibers on the underside. They accepted the gift, placing it not over but beside their own heart.

"So, where are you headed?"

"I'm not sure," I confessed. "I just figured, since this line goes to the beach…"

"Not a bad choice on a day you leave work, even if it's a little cold. But you know, you should get off three stops before the end of the line."

"Yeah?"

"There's a beach there, too—smaller, not as popular, but it's near a couple of local farms. You can pick some pumpkins."

"Pumpkins?"

They shrugged again. "'Tis the season."

"I guess it is."

I gazed out the window at the ombré foliage, starting in low tones of crisp, dead brown through violent reds into high notes of pale yellow. There didn't seem to be any green left, and I found that strangely comforting, as though I had a temporary embargo on the color: the only green in the world would come in the form of stickers, and I was their keeper.

"This is me," they announced as the train slowed to a halt.

"Sorry about your brother," I finally said, though I knew the sentiment was late. In a way, I felt I meant it more now that we'd taken a ride together.

"Thanks," they responded, but gestured to the sticker as the words left their mouth, and I wondered what they were offering gratitude for.

"I'll leave an extra pumpkin on my seat on the way back," I found myself telling them as they stood to leave.

"I'll look for it when I head home," they promised, waving goodbye as they got off at their stop.

The tracks ahead, though they were invisible to me, seemed to yawn on for ages, the train moving quickly but taking forever. I wondered how my coworker was faring with her not-nice-guy harassment situation, and felt a spark of hope: perhaps I had inspired a walkout. I might be failing as a writer, but there were other ways to reach people.

I almost missed the stop the person I'd met had suggested, not sure whether to take their advice. But as I hesitated, looking uncertainly at the platform, I remembered my promise of a pumpkin and stepped down just as the doors slid closed behind me.

The farm with the pumpkins was apparently a popular destination. The second person I asked about it pointed me there, and it would have been a fifteen-minute walk if I hadn't stopped for something warm to drink on my way.

"'Tis the season," I said after I'd asked the server behind the counter for a caramel apple latte. It would have been needlessly sweet, but I got a triple shot and figured I could ride the sugar-caffeine high for the rest of the afternoon, until the anxiety at having basically told my entire office to fuck itself really set it.

There was nothing immediately remarkable about the place. It looked like any local farm stand, with a small indoor space for people to go to the bathroom and pay for little harvest souvenirs and ornaments, priced up because they claimed to be handmade. I thought that maybe some of them even were.

When I approached the pumpkin stand, I found a group of people gathered around with confused looks on their faces, but no pumpkins. One woman in her fifties was making apologies to a couple with a small boy.

"There's another stand a few miles north of here," she told them. "We hate to send away business, but it looks like whoever took them left none behind."

"I just don't get it. Fucking weird." This from a guy about my age, maybe a few years younger, whose remarks earned him a dirty look from the older woman, I assumed on account of the language he'd used in front of the kid.

I'd read somewhere that people who swear tend to be more trustworthy than people who don't. "What happened?" I asked the guy as I approached.

He shrugged, gesturing around the barren stand. "Someone apparently stole every last pumpkin we had for sale, although I don't know how they could've gotten very far with them."

"What makes you say that?" This was the most interesting thing that had happened in my vicinity all week. I wasn't about to apologize for my curiosity.

"Well, we've got cameras on the driveway and parking lot. There were no cars during the night—I checked the footage myself. Whoever took them would have had to do so on foot."

"Could've used a wheelbarrow," another woman, also around our age, guessed. "Or a cart of some kind."

"I don't see any tracks." He raised a dubious eyebrow at her. "The whole thing is just fucking weird."

"What's that?" I asked, noticing a tall structure a couple of hundred feet away. It looked like a corn maze, except... "It's massive."

"Oh, that's Bobby's maze," the young woman who'd mentioned carts smiled. "He builds one every year—outdoes himself each fall."

"How so?"

"It gets bigger and more difficult every time." The guy rolled his eyes. "We've actually had to implement a minimum age limit because we had so many kids getting stuck and having meltdowns in the past."

I snorted, amused. "It's really that hard?"

"Oh, you'll get your ten bucks' worth, if you're planning on trying it," the woman grinned at me. "But I wouldn't go in on an empty stomach or with a full bladder."

Feeling that my body currently contained neither of those inhibitors, I dug a ten-dollar bill out of my pocket and handed it to her.

"Good luck," she said, her companion shaking his head and muttering about the fucked-up day as he wandered off into the farm shop. I turned in the opposite direction, making a beeline for this exalted cornstalk structure.

When you walk into a maze made of corn that's taller than you, your world becomes strangely hushed. Not silent, because you hear the constant rustle of leaves in the wind all around you, but the sounds of the world outside the labyrinth are muffled. I thought suddenly that if there were a maze like this at work, I might not need my frowning stickers.

I could hear myself breathe. More than that, I heard myself think. They weren't thoughts that were trying to drown out something dreadful; they were thoughts of their own. And I realized that I hadn't been anywhere really quiet in a long time, especially not a place to be with my thoughts and write.

"Day-after-ditching-work goals," I decided out loud, feeling calm enough to think about tomorrow for the first time since I'd left the office.

I turned another corner and was starting to wonder if I might end up like one of the little kids that panicked after being stuck for too long in the maze, but out of nowhere, a clearing appeared. It looked as though someone had meticulously vandalized the maze, carefully knocking over cornstalk walls within a small space so that the pathways around the area were still intact. There, where a section of maze had once stood, was a pile of at least forty or fifty neatly stacked pumpkins.

"So this is where they went." My voice got an unexpected response from the pile, a small yelping that wasn't like any sound I'd ever heard a pumpkin make.

I approached, my curiosity again getting the better of me. And I found, on the opposite side of the pumpkin pile, a small brown-and-black dachshund, wagging its tail in a friendly but slightly desperate way.

"How did you get here?" I asked, reaching out to lift him. I received another yelp for my troubles, and then he licked my face a few times and settled in my arms.

Figuring it was safer to go back the way I'd come into the maze than try to figure out which of the other paths from the clearing might lead to an exit, I set the dog down and picked out two pumpkins that were small enough to carry. With very little prompting, I was able to get the dog to follow me, closely enough that I started calling him Shadow.

When we emerged and I returned to the young woman I'd been talking to, her mouth fell open. "Where did you get that?"

"He followed me from inside the maze. I think he was lost in there for a while."

"No," she shook her head, "I mean the pumpkins!"

"Oh, yeah—can I buy these two? I'm pretty sure they're the ones you're supposed to be selling. There's like forty or so more in the center of the maze."

"*What?*" She turned to the older woman. "Debbie! This girl found all of our pumpkins!"

"Where?" The older woman came over, a relieved look on her face.

"They're in the middle of the corn maze," I told her.

"Bobby's maze?" Her eyebrows shot up.

"That's what I said!" the younger woman replied. "I'll go get Tom. He's not going to believe this."

Tom, the guy who'd spoken to me earlier, couldn't believe it. Or rather, he "couldn't fucking believe it," which earned him a smack on the head from Debbie.

I helped them move the pumpkins, which took a few trips because the paths of the maze were too narrow for any kind of cart to come through, further debunking the younger woman's earlier speculations. I learned her name was Jill.

"How the hell did someone manage to get every single pumpkin in here?" Tom asked exasperatedly during our third trip into the maze.

Shadow was waiting patiently for me outside the maze entrance. He had fun escorting us back to the pumpkin stand each time we emerged, but clearly had no interest in getting lost inside the cornstalks again.

"Are you all sure he doesn't belong to anyone? Maybe a neighbor?" I asked.

Debbie assured me he didn't. "He really seems to like you, though. Want a leash for him? We've got an extra collar from when our Charlene was a puppy—I bet it could fit him."

I was generously gifted the lead and collar for Shadow, which were a striking shade of hot pink. Shadow looked handsome in his new gear, and I was given the two pumpkins free of charge, despite my protests.

"You spared us more of Tom's grumbling than we would've heard without your help moving them," Jill reassured me. "And you're the one who found the pile in the first place."

I asked if they could point me in the direction of the beach, and holding Shadow's leash in one hand and a bag with my two small pumpkins in the other, I left the farm just in time to hear Tom cursing a shelf in the shop that had come loose.

The walk was more pleasant because I had Shadow for company. Ten minutes in, I realized this dog was absolutely mine. That gave me a bizarre sort of revelation: I was no longer an unhappy, unpublished writer. I was Shadow's human and I had somewhere to be, at least for the evening. I decided that this change was working for me.

We got to the beach as the sun was just starting to set, and apparently it was too cold for anyone else, because we found ourselves alone. But the person on the train had been right—it was nicer than the bigger beach I'd initially intended to visit.

Shadow was not interested in the cold water in the slightest. When I took off my jacket and shoes, he settled down on the sand patiently, apparently ready to wait as his new owner continued being her strange self.

The water was freezing, and I shivered with my first steps in. But I didn't feel cold in the way that usually leaves me searching for a heater or a blanket. It was a sharp feeling, and I walked into it until I was swimming under the surface. I knew I couldn't stay for long, given how cold it would be on the walk back to the train. The sun would've had to be out to give me a fighting chance at not getting sick.

But for the moment, I was interested in how loose my limbs were starting to feel. I couldn't sense my fingertips or my toes anymore, and I wanted to surface less and less the longer I stayed under. I found myself rolling over continuously under the water—on my back, then facedown, face up, turn down—but on one such rotation, lights seemed to appear above, and I worried that maybe the cold had induced some kind of shock. I surfaced.

There was a girl standing a few feet into the water, no more than fourteen or fifteen years old. She was holding what looked to be a bunch of floating Christmas lights at first glance, and then I realized they were clear balloons with lights encircling them, extending down their strings into her hands. She had red wellies on so that her feet stayed dry, and she was staring at me, a frown on her face just like the one on my stickers.

"Hi."

She didn't respond for a second, just raised a skeptical eyebrow at me. It struck me as funny that she was the age I'd been when I started to write.

"I like those balloons."

She looked up at them, then back at me. "What's wrong with you?"

"It was a bad day." I realized I was in a low squat, the waves bobbing me up and down, but I didn't want to stand because I knew I'd be even colder the moment I did. "I'm getting over it."

"I get that," she replied after a moment. "I mean, I guess I do."

I nodded, waiting for her to leave. She seemed to understand, because she let out a sigh and turned to go. Before she walked away, she asked, "Is that your dog?"

I nodded again, a smile I hadn't expected crossing my face.

"He's cute." With that, she did leave. I took one more long dive under the waves, then decided the ten or fifteen minutes I'd spent in freezing autumn water was probably enough for a cold to set in, even pneumonia if I should be so unlucky.

Standing, I thought for a moment that the girl was waiting on the beach because my eyes met the same floating lights. But she'd just left a balloon behind, tied to Shadow's collar. He barked at me a couple of times, as though to remind me that I was being fucking nihilistic and enough was enough.

"I hear you, pup." I wrung my hair and clothing out best I could as I trudged towards my new companion and his bright balloon. After I'd put my jacket and shoes back on, my teeth chattering in the evening breeze, we began heading back to the train.

I remembered to leave a pumpkin on a seat, and I hoped the person I'd met earlier that day would pick it up on the way back from the hospital. I tied the balloon to its stem.

On the long ride back, as I eased into the blessedly heated train car with Shadow sitting next to me, I hatched what seemed like an ingenious plan, or at least a workable one. The next day, I would go to the startup office across the hall with a solution for their neurotic dachshund problem: since he was the only one of his breed in their office, that dog apparently felt the need to act out. And that was understandable. So, maybe they weren't hiring at the moment, but then, maybe a position could be found for an employee with strong writing skills, great taste in coffee, and a very well-adjusted dachshund who could keep their errant pissing puppy company at the office.

It was worth a shot, right?

Song and Siren

The house was built over a period of seven weeks, and during that time it rained more than once. Nothing protected the foundation from dampness, so as they continued to build, there was no line of defense against the mold.

It wasn't surprising, then, that the first four tenants died not long after moving in. Though their deaths were the result of the toxic stuff in the walls, neighbors murmured their fears of a house no one could survive, stories of ghosts they'd heard as children rolling through their minds as they drank their evening tea and kissed their beloveds goodnight.

Spring was not far off when she moved in, but the air held a persistent chill. She became ill like the others, but already two months pregnant, her body was ready to thrive. And so, despite cold air and walls full of mold, she did not die. Instead, she warmed the house with lamps that shone in the night, bathtubs full of steaming rose water, and velvety throws that soothed the wooden furniture, quieting painful memories of glowing pasts as oaks and pines. At times, she heard sounds like dreams of distant forests, much warmer than this strange house that smelled of mold.

It was spring when the mermaid song began from inside her belly, some weeks before it would resound in the open air. She stroked the keys of the piano, its tones pleasantly muffled by a periwinkle throw. Though the sounds were dampened by distance, the little boy in the next house heard them. The smell of the furniture also drifted across the yard, the scents of pine and oak telling him of better lives. And like those wooden benches and heavy bookshelves, the only joy the boy knew came in quiet, amniotic tones that blended beautifully with the notes of a muted piano.

Her lungs were weak from the mold, but not those of her own little mermaid, who burst forth in a sea of salted blood, who warmed the house more than lamps and throws could ever do. The little girl sang with lungs full of vitality. Her voice traveled into the neighbors' houses at night, and their fears of ghosts melted into dreams of a darkly welcoming sea. The trees that lived along the street flourished: by the time she learned to play the piano herself, they had more than doubled the breadth of their branches.

And when the boy next door began loading the gun, he heard her voice. Turning from the violence he'd planned, he caught sight of her through a window, singing to furniture that mourned the forest, its home and its kindred. The boy's hands shook; the bullets fell. Instead of bending to retrieve them, he packed the few things in the world that mattered to him and left, never to return. The song of a ghost-banishing siren filled his ears for the rest of his life, driving him to the forest and the sea.

FISSURES

Honey

The first thing I can remember from the accident is the sound: it came to me in the form of light.

They told us later that the sirens on the squad cars and the ambulance had been turned off because they hadn't wanted to disturb us with the noise, as if noise could do more damage than shattered glass, than ash falling onto shattered feelings of: *I know where we are; I remember who I am.*

But I don't know that I could have even heard the sirens, because those flashing lights played so loudly in my ears I could feel the very shadows in the space between them, where blood vessels and brain tissue were supposed to be. I smelled nothing, tasted nothing; I'm sure my eyes were open, but have no memory of anything passing before them.

If I saw anything, it was the illumination of my mind as that endless song of light ran relentless between my ears. It was the sound of emergency. The world had receded hours before, and I was caught in sonic chaos: terror, knowledge unspeakable, light.

*   *   *

My uncle had been threatening to cut us off for years. As self-important as supporting his younger brother's family made him feel, that sentiment was tempered by monetary loss. I don't think my father or brothers ever believed he would actually make good on his threats. But I remembered the last piece of life wisdom my mother gave me before she left us: "Whether you're hearing promises or threats, you need to watch your back if it's a man doing the talking."

I still remember how she looked when she said this, the light of the setting sun making her cherry lipstick blister like a child's balloon across her mouth, her sunglasses casting huge copper light-shadows over her cheeks and eyes. I was twelve, sitting beside her in the front seat of her veritable boat of a car. A couple of months later, all three of them were gone: car, mother, and color-casting sun.

Our family, those of us who remained—my father, my little brother Matt, my older brother Charlie, and me—were the sort of people you might call ambulance chasers. Dad took jobs here and there fixing up properties. This work would come in the wake of someone else's tragedy: bank foreclosures, desertions, evictions, sudden deaths. He always did a lovely job; you can't imagine such precision and artistry until you've seen it firsthand, and to look at what Dad would create was to admire a domestic masterpiece. But the work was always a beautiful façade built on some stranger's misery, and that knowledge took its toll.

Charlie worked at a local scrap yard, and after school, I volunteered with an animal rescue group. The rescue dealt with a lot of old people who had to give up their pets because they were being forced into senior homes. Sometimes, we even went door-to-door visiting older folks with cats or dogs, pretending to ask for donations but really checking on "how many crayons short of a full box they might be," as the head of the rescue group put it.

I hated those visits. On some level, I knew that every time old Mrs. Whatshername invited me in for tea and couldn't find the sugar bowl on the table right in front of her, I was feeling the way my father did when he looked for work in neighborhoods where big banks had a new foothold. But I knew my boss wanted what was best for the animals, just like my dad wanted what was best for me, Charlie, and Matt.

We weren't doing great after my mother left. She was the most capable member of the family. That's not to say that the rest of us weren't hardworking, or that we were dull. But my mother had always been exceptional. Dad said she was charmed. Any project she undertook was an instant success; any person she met longed to be in her good graces; any clothing she wore looked stunning on her; any simple household chore was executed as a work of art. Our houseplants spilled off of windowsills and grew wild across the patio and the porch, thriving when everyone else's plants on our street suffered from pests or disease. Comforting breezes blew through our home on the most humid days. Our bedsheets were always cool, our towels never lost their fluff, and I don't remember a speck of dust ever managing to linger in the house long enough for me to notice it. Local dogs rolled over when my mother walked by; cats ran to rub up against her legs; even the birds and insects seemed to like hanging around our place.

And, of course, any man she met fell in love with her on sight.

*   *   *

"Edna."

It was my uncle's voice on the phone. I said nothing but kept the receiver to my ear and mouth as though I meant to.

"Edna, is that you? I can hear you breathing, honey. Let me speak with your father."

No response from me.

I could hear my uncle hesitate, and his voice got a little lower, a little huskier as he spoke again. "...Lillian?"

I slammed the phone down. That I breathed enough like my mother to be mistaken for her was a possibility I wasn't ready to accept.

She'd been gone two months. The previous week, my uncle's wife Lydia, in chronic pain since she'd driven herself drunk off a road three years prior, had remarked "how much Edna is beginning to look like Lillian." Lydia had always been nasty and bitter, even before her injury. She'd never allowed us to call her "aunt," not considering us her relations just because we were her husband's. Her words wore a thin mask of endearment, but were intended to hurt. Instead of causing me pain, though, the comment made me feel as though I'd taken a step back and my family was further away than they'd been just a moment before.

My father and uncle had regarded me silently in response to Lydia's observation. "She certainly is," my uncle agreed while my father kept quiet, and that gap between myself and the rest of them expanded. My brother Charlie left the room.

Now, hearing my uncle call me by my mother's name, having him mistake my silence for hers, I felt a new distance begin to grow. This one lived between my heart and my stomach.

The phone rang again, and I picked up. "This is Edna. It's Edna."

"Hi, sweetie! I'm glad I caught you."

I recognized Eleanor's voice, a woman who worked with me at the animal rescue. My body relaxed, and I realized I'd been gripping the phone so tightly that my hand ached.

"Do you think you can go pay Mrs. Stephenson a visit?" Eleanor went on. "She hasn't been feeling well, and her daughter is concerned about Mugsby."

Mugsby was a terrier-mix about as old and frail as his owner. I was used to routinely checking in on him and Mrs. Stephenson.

"Sure, Eleanor. I just finished my homework. I'll walk over once I make Matt a snack."

"Thank you, darling."

As I made a line of frozen chicken nuggets across a scuffed metal tray, I reflected on how Eleanor had

stopped calling me by my name since my mother had left.
I'd become "sweetheart" and "darling" and "honey"
instead of Edna. It had occurred to me that this might be
because Eleanor was worried no one would call me these
things anymore, since they were terms a mother might
use. I didn't know how to tell her that my mother had
called me by my name or not at all. I don't think the word
"honey" had ever passed her lips, except to say that she
would have none in her tea.

After they'd warmed for a few minutes in the oven,
I threw the defrosted nuggets onto a navy-blue plate and
brought them to Matt's room. In the unlit hall, the plate
was so dark that the nuggets seemed to float between my
hands. Blue was Matt's favorite color, and though the
two of us should have fought like cats and dogs according
to what I'd seen in other families, I liked to make him
smile. Charlie had always been a good big brother to me,
and besides, Matt was only ten; if I hadn't been nice to
him, I would have felt like a bully.

The light in his room made the plate visible once
more. I found him playing a video game. He didn't look
up when I entered, but I was thinking about both phone
calls and didn't really notice. I put the nuggets on a table
and said over my shoulder as I left the room, "I'll be home
in like an hour, but Charlie and Dad might beat me back.
Make sure you eat those before they get here or they
might swap them out for some veggies."

I stepped out into the heat of late afternoon,
preparing myself for the visit to Mrs. Stephenson. I knew

that she probably wasn't doing well, and I had to prepare myself for the sad scene that awaited me.

Something irritating was playing over and over in my head as I walked along the broken sidewalk, dodging cracks and tree roots. It was an annoying sequence of beeps and tones, though the hot day around me was quiet except for insects and the noise of passing cars. Still, the sound wouldn't leave my mind. I thought of busy signals, text notifications, and dial tones before I realized it was the music that had been playing in the background of Matt's video game. It followed me all the way to Mrs. Stephenson's, no matter how many tunes I hummed in an attempt to get rid of it.

*   *   *

It was Matt, not me, who was the core of our family's collateral damage. Poor Matt, only a couple of years younger than I was but so far behind me in grasping solid ground again after our mother had gone.

He stopped speaking when she left. We didn't notice, at first. He'd been quiet from the time he was small, and we were in such collective disarray after her departure—my father trying to figure out money, Charlie shouldering extra shifts and allowing his schoolwork to become less and less of a priority. By the time we realized that no words had left my baby brother's mouth since his mother had gone, it already seemed far too late.

And I suppose it was, because the accident happened and the world fell to pieces, and it could have been stopped if we had simply asked him what he was doing when he played around on the computer, what he was reading when he wasn't doing his homework, and what he was thinking when he figured that the old gas stove in our kitchen might be something to mess around with.

*   *   *

"Mrs. Stephenson?" I knocked at the door, watching chips of paint fall from the timid impact of my knuckles. I had to knock two more times, increasing the pressure with which I rapped at the wood and peeling paint. Finally, Mrs. Stephenson came to the door and invited me in for soda and cookies.

We sat at the table, and I answered the usual questions about school and my brothers. Finally, I had to ask, "So, how's Mugsby? I haven't seen him yet today—is he outside?"

Mrs. Stephenson frowned at me. "You know, dear, I know that Sophie put you up to this."

Sophie was Mrs. Stephenson's daughter. I knew that if my visit caused any family problems, I would get a talking-to from Eleanor. I tried to backtrack from the initial question. "Oh, I just really like Mugsby, Mrs. Stephenson. We've never been able to have a dog, and—"

"It's not nice to lie, dear," Mrs. Stephenson cut me off. Her frown had deepened, and her eyes were wide. "It's bad enough to have a daughter who doesn't care to visit or call. The fact that she sends someone else's daughter to come to her mother's home asking about a dog and not her mother—"

"Really, Mrs. Stephenson, I haven't even spoken to Sophie," I attempted weakly, telling whatever truth I thought might help.

"Don't you cut me off!" Her voice had turned nasty. "You're rude and careless, just like your mother. Lillian was thoughtless and she raised a bad girl, and bad girls stick together, don't they? That's how you and Sophie have found one another."

I couldn't speak, recoiling from the table, but she grabbed my wrist with a spotted hand. I was shocked that a grip so strong could come from arthritic knuckles warped with age.

"Bad mothers raise bad girls," she continued, not letting go of my wrist or allowing my gaze to break from hers. "I suppose Lillian and I had that in common."

I felt tears coming forth. I hadn't cried since my mother had left, but here this strange woman was, making my mouth tremble. I could hear Mugsby barking loudly from the next room, sensing his owner's distress.

Mrs. Stephenson threw my wrist away from her, so hard that my hand smacked painfully against the table, knocking over the soda glass.

"Look at this mess," she remarked, her voice calm as it had been when we'd started our conversation. "No wonder Lillian left you."

I ran from the house. I could feel my blood pulsing through my ears, pounding so hard it made me dizzy. My father's car intercepted me on the way home, with Charlie and Dad listening to old songs I didn't know on the radio. I climbed into the back seat, grateful that we were not the kind of family that would ask one another how the day had gone.

*   *   *

I'm still not sure why she left. My memory of being twelve years old, apart from that explosive day two months after she'd gone, is fragmented at best. I'm sure it's from the shock of losing her, although I don't find it painful to think about.

I don't so much recall her leaving as I remember life in the wake of her, when the plants started to die, and the house became messy, and my father started having long and humiliating phone calls with my uncle, one of many men to cast his eyes towards my mother despite the fact that she was his little brother's wife.

In a way, the night of the accident ended something that my mother's leaving had started. Maybe that's why I don't need clear memories of whatever pain or sadness it caused. Maybe that night, the strange ending that was that night, suffices in the mosaic of my twelve-year-old mind for memories and devastation.

I do recall that sometimes in the days right after she'd left, if I closed my eyes tightly I could hear my mother's voice sounding through the halls of our modest home. This happened mostly at dawn, when the sun-kissed hope that day brings would proceed slowly through the house, a timid glow that expands so softly it could drown you and you would never see it coming. The sound wasn't happy, though even now, I always feel sweetness when I think of her; like the men whose disappointed hopes trailed her vanishing silhouette, I've never been immune to the spell my mother cast.

But the sound of her voice haunted me. It was the part of me that couldn't quite let go of whatever had made her leave, the wicked catalyst that destroyed my father and the household we had loved, even before the accident expelled us into uncharted misery.

*   *   *

"Edna. Edna. Honey, can you talk to us? Can you say anything to us, Edna?"

I remember thinking in frustration, *Why can't the world decide whether to call you honey or by your name?* These words were the first things I heard beyond the light, and they made no sense to me.

"Edna." The paramedic who'd been calling my name and shining a light in my face was persistent. "Please, talk to us if you can."

"What happened?" I managed. It seemed like a good question to ask.

"There was an accident, honey."

"My name is not honey," I told her. "My mother hated honey. I'm Edna."

It would be two days before we could see Matt in the hospital. In the span of just two hours, though, the roof of the house caved in, and there was nothing left to save.

*   *   *

We are so lucky, everyone tells us to this very day. None of us died. Matt didn't die, and he could have in so many ways, even before the explosion.

The firefighters investigated. I remember the fact that our mother had left was suspect, or rather, it made my father a suspect, because it meant our home was not harmonious. That was the word one of the social workers used—"harmonious," as though a family should be making music.

It wasn't harmonious in that house, though. Before the aural distress of the explosion and the mute echo of crisis that followed, there had been no song in our home. When I think of that voice that followed me after she left, those muted echoes trailing through the house, nothing happy or melliferous comes to mind. That sound haunting me before each dawn, sweet though its presence may have seemed at the time—that sound was cold, chilling, void of light.

The Tuesday Murders

What began as an innocuous foray into the study of a particular subspecies of mushroom resulted in a total of twenty-two murders. And the way she would tell it later, it was clear that everything could have been avoided if the stupid mushrooms hadn't shown up in the first place, but apparently there was no stopping fungus from popping up wherever it felt like popping up.

It was, in the end, quite similar to those people she'd found the need to murder, though as with the mushrooms, her efforts never seemed to take.

*   *   *

Katrina Wells woke up on a Tuesday morning to find a mushroom growing in her apartment.

"How?" she demanded, not having more words available for the moment. She'd gotten considerably drunk the evening before, because although it had been a Monday, it had also been the last night of a three-day weekend. And while Trina didn't have much to celebrate, it was the principle of the thing: three-day weekends meant alcohol, just as autumn meant sweaters and funerals meant wearing black. Trina had always been one to stand on principle.

Her hangover was palpable. Her head was throbbing and her tongue seemed to have taken residence at the very front of her mouth, so the sight of a mushroom growing on the side of the central weight-bearing pillar in the middle of her studio apartment was unwelcome, to say the least.

"You'd think this was a goddamned tree in the middle of a forest," she griped aloud as she went to remove the mushroom.

Unlike most mushrooms Trina had encountered up to that point in her life, though, this was not a delicate, easily crumbled piece of fungus. This sucker held fast, and Trina ended up hacking away at it with the sharpest knife in her kitchen. And even though the blows were intense and the blade more than adequate, there was left behind a lump of nastiness that she'd have to contend with when she returned home from work.

"All of this before coffee," she muttered, heading to the shower only to find that, without warning, her building had again shut off the hot water.

                    *   *   *

Kirk and Sean were exactly the kind of asshats Trina tried to avoid in life, but since the renovations had begun in her office, they were now part of her cubicle cluster. She'd spent the better part of the past two weeks trying to contain herself amidst lewd jokes, loud belches, lengthy conversations with her breasts, the cleaning up of messes she hadn't been the one to make, and more condescending mansplanations than she'd ever received in her life (all regarding things that she knew perfectly well how to do, naturally).

Today, though, Sean had apparently gotten bored avoiding the work he was paid more than his female colleagues to do, and so he waited until Trina had gone to the bathroom and as she came out, opened what was a warm and recently shaken can of soda all over the white blouse she'd been wearing.

"What do you mean, I can't go home and change?" Trina asked Becky, the office manager, working not to grit her teeth as she spoke.

"Well, like, I can't just let people leave the office whenever they feel like it. I mean, it is your *job*."

"Which you expect me to do covered in someone else's soda?"

"I mean, I can't be responsible for you not looking where you're going when you leave the bathroom, Katrina."

"I already told you, Sean clearly—"

Becky wrinkled her nose in what she evidently thought was an endearing manner. Trina hadn't felt the urge to hit someone since middle school, but it seemed as though she had spent the past two weeks keeping her hands from forming fists. It was one reason she was still a touch hungover now.

"Aw, those guys don't mean anything. They just like to blow off steam to make the work go by more quickly. They're really great guys."

"I guess I wouldn't know."

"Well, we can't stand around here chatting all day. Work needs to get done once in a while, right?" Becky smiled brightly but pointedly at Trina, who heard a distinct set of snickers sounding from behind her.

Great. She had an audience.

"Fine, Becky."

As she turned to walk away, Sean passed her on his way to Becky's desk and said, his tone so sincere she could've sunk her nails into his voice box, "I had no idea that would be your only shirt, Trina. So sorry you didn't see me."

"Yeah, that's what happened, Sean."

He shook his head as he walked towards Becky's desk. As Trina left, she heard him saying, "I honestly try to get along with everyone here, Becks."

"Some people just like to hold grudges," Becky replied, clicking her tongue soothingly.

Irene, the closest thing Trina had to a friend in the office, gave her a look of quiet fury as she returned to her cube. "I have no idea how you didn't slap her. That woman wouldn't know solidarity if it bit her in the ass."

"I could care less about Becky," Trina replied, and it was true. "It's not her fault that she wasn't there the day they gave out personalities. It's the company she keeps that I take issue with."

Irene nodded. "These office renovations can't get done soon enough," she agreed. "Well, at least this will mark one less day we have to spend around those assholes, right?"

*   *   *

When she finally got out of work, Trina had to duck into a budget shop around the corner and buy a five-dollar t-shirt. She didn't have the time to run home or the cash to spend anywhere else, and if she was late to meet Ginny, she'd never hear the end of it.

Ginny and Trina had been friends since their mandatory science credit in college, which they helped each other pass (though neither managed to do particularly well). They met for dinner regularly, and more often than not, Ginny had some loser in tow who she expected Trina to socialize with and approve of. A week or two afterwards, Trina would receive a tearful phone call, and she'd end up buying drinks to comfort her old friend.

It was a truly exhausting cycle, one she'd been intending to break for the past three years, except who the hell had the kind of time to actually work on their relationships with other people? In the meantime, Trina had taken to holding her breath whenever she was meeting up with Ginny and praying for a normal, friends-only dinner.

But as she entered the restaurant wearing a bright Hello Kitty t-shirt tucked into her pencil skirt, she saw with a single glance that tonight she was going to be a third wheel once again.

"For fuck's sake, this day will not quit," she muttered as she pushed through the crowded restaurant, and an old woman looked up at the sound of her voice.

"You're telling me, honey," the woman said. "Two of my best friends dropped dead this week, one in the middle of bingo. She was on a winning streak, too. And I'm guessing from that t-shirt that you've got some pretty valid complaints yourself."

Trina blinked down at her, not sure what to say. Sure, the commiseration was nice, although she could've done without the overshare about dead friends. She settled on, "Thanks? I mean, I'm also sorry."

"Eh, I'm used to it. I decided a while ago that I'd outlive all those assholes."

Before she could figure out what to say beyond that, she heard Ginny's high-pitched voice rise above the bustle of the restaurant. "Trina! Trina, we're right over here!"

"Good grief, do you hear the lungs on that one?" Trina heard the woman saying as she continued on her way. "I wouldn't want to live next-door to that during mating season."

"Hey, Trina!" Ginny beamed up at her. "This is Chet. Chet, meet Trina."

Trina had to hand it to Ginny: although it was completely impossible that he would not turn out to be a loser like all the others, Chet was staggeringly good-looking. He was the kind of good-looking that had Trina actually a little jealous of Ginny, which almost never happened because what a fucking train wreck. He was the kind of good-looking that made Trina want to pull him into the bathroom with his belt in her teeth. In fact, he was the kind of good-looking that elicited wolf whistles from old ladies, because that was what snapped

Trina out of her stupor and got her to sit down at the table like a human being.

"Hey, Chet," she said. "It's good to meet you, I'm sure."

He gave a nod in her direction. "Nice shirt."

This day would just not fucking end.

*   *   *

On her way to her apartment building from the parking lot, Trina ran into Todd, which was the absolute last thing she could have hoped for on what was proving to be the worst Tuesday she could recall experiencing in a very long time, if ever.

"Hey! Hey, Trina, how are ya?"

Unlike the irreverent woman Trina had encountered at the restaurant who was actually a senior citizen, Todd spoke and acted like he'd been on the planet for several decades, but he was Trina's age, possibly a little younger. On top of that, he'd made his very awkward crush on her very awkwardly clear from the day she'd moved into the building.

"Well, to be honest, Todd, I'm not doing great. Really looking forward to heading home and shutting out the day and everyone in it, you know what I mean?"

He let out an actual guffaw, not for the first time since she'd known him. Trina had to remind herself that she was not wearing sunglasses because it was nighttime and an eyeroll would be inappropriate and probably a little mean. And while Todd had not ever done anything deserving of her kindness, she knew that anyone who encountered her this evening would only be receiving the brunt of her feelings about the day, and that didn't seem fair.

But Todd also could not take a hint, something she'd been reminded of every time she had run into him, which was too often.

"Yeah, yeah, I hear ya!"

"That's nice, Todd. Have a good night."

"I'll walk you to your door."

"I really wish you wouldn't."

"No trouble at all!" He shoved himself in front of her to open the lobby door and missed popping her in the face with it by less than an inch.

"Really, Todd," Trina said, feeling her teeth gritting together in spite of her efforts to remain politic, "I'll be fine going to my apartment the way I do every single day after work."

"But you're home late tonight, Trina," he insisted as he trailed her towards the split in the lobby that led to her side of the building rather than his own.

Trina's eyes narrowed. "Excuse me?"

"I mean, you're usually back three hours before this. It's late, and you shouldn't—"

"Why do you know my schedule, Todd?" she asked, her voice growing hard.

He stopped, his expression like an animal caught in headlights. There was an aspect of the pathetic about him, but she didn't have the energy for pity and wasn't sure that Todd had even earned it. Keeping tabs on her comings and goings went beyond awkward: it was downright creepy.

Taking advantage of his flustered state, she allowed her tone to turn snappish. "Like I said, I'm looking forward to being alone now. Goodnight, Todd." And she walked hurriedly to her apartment, expertly shoved her keys in the locks, and slammed the door and clicked it shut before anyone or anything else from this day could follow her inside.

*   *   *

"What?" Trina groaned as she woke up, head pounding and mouth parched. "*Why*?"

She'd been delighted to go to bed the previous night. Wednesday would *have* to be better than the completely awful start of her work week. And even if it wasn't a huge improvement, the three-day weekend ensured less time until Friday rolled around.

But Trina could not fathom why she'd woken up feeling completely hungover. She'd only had one glass of wine at dinner with Ginny and Chet. Why was her skull punishing her like this?

As she blinked her bleary eyes, she saw that the mushroom had returned; in fact, it had brought company, as two distinct little caps were sitting on the side of the weight-bearing pillar.

She pushed herself out of bed, got the knife she'd used the previous morning, and resumed hacking away. The mushrooms proved difficult to get rid of once more, and, glancing at the clock, Trina lost the hope she'd been harboring of having coffee before work.

Muttering to herself about fungus, she stumbled to the bathroom. When she stepped into the shower, she found that the hot water was off.

"This again?!" she shrieked, shivering as she scrubbed herself with ice water for the second morning in a row. Wednesday was already proving to be as much of a bitch as its predecessor; worse, even, because she'd already had to suffer through such a morning before.

*   *   *

Trina felt something was strange when she got to the office. For one thing, Irene asked her how her weekend was.

"Good," Trina said, trying to keep her bewilderment at the question from entering her voice. After all, she certainly knew what it was like to lose track of the days.

But then she found herself the victim of another warm can of soda upon leaving the bathroom. She glared at Sean and snapped, "Seriously? Again? What, do you not know any other form of office prank?"

His usual dickbag grin turned into a look of judgment not unlike the one she'd found herself holding back constantly this week. "You all right there, Wells? I didn't know you were coming out of the bathroom, or I'd—"

"Yeah, yeah, whatever." She stalked back to her desk, not bothering with Becky.

"Are you okay?" Irene asked her, alarmed.

"I mean, I'm getting sick and tired of this shit," she replied, releasing some of the edge from her voice so that she didn't take her anger out on Irene. "Other than that, just generally annoyed with everything, I guess?"

"Don't you want to talk to Becky about it?"

Trina rolled her eyes. "What for? We both know what she's going to say."

"We do?" Irene looked genuinely puzzled, and Trina let out a sigh.

"Look, Irene, I know you think women should support women and all that, but do you really think Becky's going to be any different than she was yesterday? She's practically sitting in Sean's lap every chance she gets."

"Yesterday? You mean Friday," Irene corrected her, and before Trina could say she damn well meant what she'd said, she went on, "but I guess you're right about her. Still, it seems horrible that you're going to have to sit there in a shirt full of soda until, what? End of day?"

"Yes," Trina blinked at her work-friend incredulously. "Yes, that does seem horrible, doesn't it?"

Irene gave her another slightly baffled look, then shrugged. "Well, I can't blame you for not wanting to try. These renovations have put stress on all of us and as far as I'm concerned, they can't get finished soon enough." She offered Trina a smile that she seemed to mean as encouraging. "And at least this marks one less day with those assholes, right?"

Trina just nodded mutely, now genuinely a little worried about Irene. Had she really forgotten their conversation from the day before? If her coworker was losing her mind, Trina didn't know where that left her. It wasn't like she could go to Becky about getting Irene help. Besides, she didn't want to risk losing the one person at the office she could stand and being left all alone, surrounded by monsters.

*   *   *

On her way out of the office, Trina's phone pinged suddenly.

Can't wait to see you!!

It was a text from Ginny.

"What the fuck?" Trina muttered. Had things gone south with Chet already? She hadn't gotten a middle-of-the-night call from Ginny and agreed to discuss heartbreak after work, had she? It might explain her feeling of being hungover, and it certainly wouldn't be the first time something had woken her up that she'd forgotten about by the next morning.

But when Ginny texted a string of silly excitement emojis, Trina realized she'd seen them before. In fact, both texts were identical to the ones Ginny had sent her on the previous day at around the same time.

For the millionth time that day, Trina sensed something was *strange*. She tried to scroll up to the texts as they had appeared the day before, but there was only a much older text from Ginny above the ones she'd just received. Thinking maybe her phone had malfunctioned, she clicked the screen off and waited a beat.

When she turned it on again, though, Trina registered the date and time display on the lock screen for the first time. According to her phone, it was still Tuesday. Or it was Tuesday again.

She started to laugh, and then that feeling that something was off about the day rose up and started to overwhelm her. She tapped the person standing nearest her with her hand, not bothering to look at who it was before she did. "What day is it?"

Kirk looked at the part of his arm she'd tapped as though she'd laced her hand with mad cow disease before touching him. "Um, Tuesday." Then he let his look of disgust morph into an obnoxious grin. "What happened, Wells? You have too wild a time last night? Doing the walk of shame *and* a wet t-shirt contest for us today, huh?"

"You're a moron," she said with no vehemence. It was more of a dismissal than anything else, an indication that she needed to process what the actual fuck was happening to her and could not be bothered with anyone or anything else while she did.

"Okay, bitch," Kirk snarled, stalking away.

The words barely reached Trina. She'd lost a day; or rather, she'd had it twice. Should she go to the hospital? She'd read something about déjà vu being a trick of the brain, and this was way more than feeling like she'd been someplace before. There was no way for a person to live a day more than once. Besides, why in the world would she relive such a horrific one?

At that moment, she received another text from Ginny. She hesitated, not sure where to go from the front of the office building where she was standing: hospital, home, or restaurant?

We're meeting at the dumpling place, right? she texted Ginny back. That was where they'd been the night before. If Ginny confirmed, it would mean...well, Trina had no idea what it would mean.

She received five thumbs-up emojis in reply. Ginny really needed to get off caffeine.

Making a decision to deal with the weirdness later, she headed for a store where she knew a frightfully cheery five-dollar Hello Kitty shirt would be waiting for her.

*   *   *

When Trina slammed the door shut behind her that night, she made a beeline for the freezer where she kept an emergency bottle of vodka. If this wasn't an emergency, she didn't know what was.

As she took her first swig from the bottle, the evening rushed through her mind. Ginny and her new dude-of-the-moment, the old lady at the restaurant, awkwardly creepy Todd: all of it had been the same. She'd even asked Chet if they hadn't met before, which resulted in him giving her the judgy look that she always had to resist wearing when meeting Ginny's paramours. As far as Trina could tell, she was the only one having round two with Tuesday.

Was she a psychic? Had she dreamt the entire day? The start of a week after a three-day weekend was always a little strange, sure: Tuesday inevitably felt like Monday, and Friday came so soon you almost didn't expect it. But this...this was like nothing she'd experienced.

The vodka was starting to take over, and she decided that whether this was one long hallucination or some kind of brain lapse, she really didn't care. It was over, and that was something she was even happier about this time around. Maybe that was what this was: a universal lesson in gratitude. She'd been cranky with her life lately. Perhaps something out there was telling her to be grateful for what she had, because it could be a fuck of a lot worse.

She fell asleep in the stupid Hello Kitty shirt, not even caring that her makeup was still on. Tomorrow would be a new day, and she could deal with the weirdness of today then.

*   *   *

The mushroom wasn't a mushroom anymore; it was a cluster, five little caps shining in the light of morning. And Trina was hungover, which she'd expected, but she wasn't wearing the Hello Kitty shirt. She was wearing the nightshirt she'd gone to bed in on Monday night.

Waking up faster than she ever had without a good cup of coffee, she grabbed her phone, then opened her laptop to be sure. She checked the world clock website, flicked on an emergency radio her mother had insisted on giving her in case all other technology failed, then turned on the TV.

It was Tuesday, all over every piece of media she turned to.

Tuesday, Tuesday, Tuesday.

Trina ran out into the hallway, nightshirt and slippers be damned. She took the lobby at a jog, then started banging on Todd's door. If anyone would open to her at this time of day, it would be the resident creeper.

"Trina! Well, this is a pleasant surprise. You look quite lovely—"

"What day is it?" she demanded.

He took a step back. "Um, well, it's Tuesday. Would you like some coffee or—"

"Fuck!" she cried, and Todd stopped talking. "Fuck, are you sure?"

"Sure about the coffee?"

She waved her hands in the air a little frantically— he was so *frustrating!*—then ran back to her own apartment and slammed the door behind her. The mushrooms were the first thing that registered, and she grabbed the knife. But as she started trying to knock the things away, the blade got stuck in their thick base, and she sliced her palm trying to free it.

"Shit!" she shrieked, grabbing a dishtowel for the blood.

The TV moved to a weather report, and the announcer said through too many perfect teeth, "We've got some beautiful sun for you this Tuesday morning, folks!"

Tuesday, Tuesday, Tuesday.

Fucking Tuesday.

"I've seen this movie," Trina said to the empty room. "And I didn't like it at all."

What was she supposed to do? How *had* that movie worked? Was she supposed to get the day right somehow, and that would let her keep moving forward? Or was this just a loop she was stuck in forever?

"Okay," she breathed. "Think, Trina. What do you do now? What do you *do*?" The blood squirting from her hand and the half-mangled mushrooms in front of her provided an odd centering effect. "First, bandage your hand. Then deal with the fact that you won't have time for coffee before work."

As she was bandaging her wound, though, a thought occurred to her: why couldn't she be late to work? In fact, she could just not go to work at all. She could stay home, have all the coffee she wanted, wait for the hot water to come back on before showering, and not leave the apartment until it was time to meet Ginny. She didn't even have to meet Ginny!

But no, she decided: this could be a three-day fluke. She couldn't just not show up to work in the hopes that tomorrow would be Tuesday again. What if it wasn't? Then she'd have suffered the worst day of her life three times in a row, and she'd be out of a job on top of it. It wasn't like Becky would vouch for her.

Three times Tuesday wasn't enough to convince Trina that things wouldn't go back to normal. She'd have to give it a full work week, at the very least: once she hit day five on loop, she'd start testing the limits and playing hooky. For now, she'd have to settle for playing along.

*   *   *

Trina was late after all, because even if it was everyone else's first Tuesday, she needed to caffeinate to do this day again and stopped at a chain café near the office. She got a passive-aggressive earful from Becky on her way in the door about wanting to look "like a team player" and whatever else the woman was rattling on about. The latte Trina had gotten was more than worth putting up with her vapid office manager.

"Katrina? Did you hear what I said?"

Shit. She'd stopped listening at a point. Quickly, she took a large sip of the latte and, cheeks full of coffee, nodded. "Mm-hmm!"

Becky gave a her a look of intense judgment, and Trina fought the urge to hold up the compact mirror she kept in her desk drawer.

"Well, okay. I'm glad you understand."

As Becky walked away, Irene leaned forward. "What in the three-day weekend has gotten into you? You're never late."

Swallowing the mouthful of latte, Trina offered her a smile. "I just really needed a coffee."

"Tell me about it. I think that's the worst part about the renovations—I miss the staff room so much!"

"Really? You think that's the worst part?" Trina looked pointedly at Kirk, whose cubicle Becky had made a stop at and who was loudly regaling her with an account of his previous night, which seemed to entail antics in a particularly exclusive bar, or...something. Trina could never really tell what he was talking about; she supposed it was her fault for never having learned to speak bro.

Irene laughed. "Good point. Any chance we'll be able to avoid those assholes entirely today, you think?"

Trina shrugged. "I have an extra shirt in my bag. I'm not worried."

And for once, she really wasn't.

*   *   *

This time, when she passed the old lady in the restaurant, Trina said, "Sorry about your tough week."

"It shows, does it?" The woman shrugged. "Fucking figures."

"I think you're handling things well. Whatever you ordered looks amazing."

"It's the special, or so the very attractive young man who took my order told me. I was kind of hoping he was the special, but like you said: it's not my week."

"Trina! Trina!" Ginny started, and Trina winced a little.

"Would you listen to the lungs on her?" The old woman shook her head in amazement.

"Unfortunately, I'm going to have to for the next hour or so," Trina stage-whispered.

"Well, sweetheart, better you than me. Go with god, or whoever you pray to that might get you out of that. You're too cute to be a third wheel, you know."

Trina thought on that. "Thanks. I think you're probably right."

"When you're as old as me, you're never wrong."

As she sat down at the table, Trina said, "Hey, Ginny. Hey, Chet."

Ginny gave her a puzzled look. "I didn't realize I told you Chet was going to be here."

"You didn't."

Now Chet looked at her. "We've met?" He let his eyes slide over her in a way that would normally have infuriated Trina, except for the fact that this was the longest day she'd ever experienced because she'd experienced it three times, and Chet was ludicrously hot. "I feel like I'd remember if we had."

"You know, I actually don't think I can answer that in a way that'll make sense."

Chet smirked, and Trina could have sworn the sides of her panties slid down an inch. She shouldn't be lusting after her friend's date, she knew. She shouldn't be letting herself grin at him like this. And she definitely should not be ignoring her friend's bewilderment while making eyes at said date.

But Ginny wasn't really that good of a friend, now Trina thought about it.

On an impulse as they ordered, Trina got a fancy cocktail for Ginny. She wasn't quite sure what she herself was planning. Usually, she only bought Ginny drinks when she had to, post-inevitable breakup.

"This was so sweet of you, Trina!" Ginny cried, diving into the drink. "It's delicious!"

"Just seltzer and lime?" Chet asked Trina as he started on his whiskey. "You abstaining or something?"

"If you woke up with the hangover I had this morning, you'd be abstaining, too."

More smirking and grinning. Ginny nervously sucked at her cocktail, seeming to sense that she no longer held the upper hand at this table, and Trina didn't bother to suggest she slow down. And when, five or so minutes later, Ginny giggled about needing to use the bathroom because of a tiny bladder, Trina realized why she'd bought her not-so-good friend that drink.

"So, Chet," she began, running her finger around the circumference of her glass's edge. "How invested in seeing this whole dinner through are you?"

He cleared his throat. "Meaning?"

"Meaning: do you want to get out of here?"

His eyebrows rose in surprise, and if Trina had been drinking, she was sure the eyes beneath them would have actually seemed to be sparkling. "Seriously? Now?"

Trina shrugged. "I don't think she'll be in there peeing forever."

The look of surprise melted into an about-to-score smirk, and Trina didn't bother to remark on it. She could always slap it off his face once they were in her apartment.

"Let's go," Chet said.

Not wanting to be as awful of a friend as she had suddenly realized Ginny was, Trina left cash for the cocktail on the table as well as for her own seltzer. She even made sure there was enough for tax and a generous tip.

As they left, the old lady winked at Trina. "Better get him out of here before that town crier in a minidress comes back."

"Next time, I'm having dinner with *you*," Trina replied.

*   *   *

The sex wasn't bad, but the exhilaration of having a naked, gorgeous man in her bed on a day that had previously ended as a shitstorm was exactly what Trina needed.

They'd barely spoken on the way to her apartment, had a near-miss with Todd in the lobby (she'd have to do something about that, eventually), and then threw themselves at each other and her bed the moment the front door shut behind them. What Chet lacked in technique he made up for in endurance, and after nearly two hours, Trina decided she was satisfied. She'd even gotten to slap him a few times.

Although it had started badly and continued to be ridiculous, she wasn't completely unhappy with how this particular Tuesday was ending. She and Chet began to doze side by side, and for the first time in three days, Trina felt a restfulness settle on her.

That was until there came a pounding on her front door, just before midnight.

"The fuck?" Chet sat up, bewildered. "I didn't come here to get roughed up by anybody's pimp."

She gave him a look of disgust. "Excuse you, asshole."

"Hey, we don't know each other."

"You know what?" She put her hand on her hip after she'd stood and tied on a robe. "You're right. We don't. Is getting roughed up by random pimps something that happens to you often, Chet?"

The banging continued, and Trina grabbed the knife from its mushroom bed, not noticing how easily it came away this time. She opened the door and let the light from the hall flood the apartment.

Todd was standing there, pale and agitated-looking.

"Is something wrong?" she asked him.

He raised a gun.

"Dude," Chet raised his hands. "I don't even know her, man."

Todd's expression seemed to twitch. "You let a stranger, Trina? You never invite me into your bed, but a stranger gets to defile you?"

Trina backed up. As she did, her eyes caught the glow of the digital clock above the kitchen stove: 11:58 p.m.

"Todd," she said, trying to keep her voice steady. "You've never even asked me out on a date. How am I supposed to know you want to sleep with me?"

"You *know*," he told her, looking incredulous. "You know exactly how I feel. Every time you pass me in the hall, every time we talk, you're trying to—"

"You approach me in the hall, Todd," she reminded him, her eyes flickering between his face and the clock. "You talk to me. You follow me."

"That's not the point!" he suddenly screamed. "*You know what you're doing to me!*"

"Yo, calm down, you fucking lunatic!" Chet interjected.

Trina rolled her eyes at him. "Okay, even if my stalker hadn't burst in here, you're never coming back. What's wrong with you?"

"What's wrong with me?" Chet demanded. "You brought a fucking knife to a gun fight! And you're just...just talking to this nutcase, for what?"

Her eyes moved back to the clock: 11:59. "For another thirty seconds, give or take," she said.

Todd seemed to realize she was doing something, and he raised the gun to her face.

"You'll save me some pain if you wait half a second, Todd," she told him. "Although I don't know if I want you to, actually. I'd appreciate a bit of a motivator, because tomorrow, I'm going to kill you right back."

The blast was shattering; the darkness, too.

And then Trina woke with a horrific hangover in the early light of Tuesday morning.

*   *   *

This time, the mushrooms had formed a definite, sizable cluster. Instead of the knife, Trina opened a cabinet and dug out the one cast iron skillet she owned and began to whack at the cluster like every single one of its little caps wore Todd's murderous face in the dark of her apartment.

It was bad enough she had a stalker, but had he seriously slut-shamed her in her own home? And in front of Chet, of all people?

"Well, I won't be doing *him* again," she remarked through gritted teeth.

Whack! One mushroom fell to the floor. *Bang!* Another two fell as she gave the weight-bearing beam a good hit. Someone pounded on the wall from the next apartment and Trina promptly screamed an invitation for them to join her fucking party. The pounding stopped and she commenced beating the shit out of the mushrooms.

When she was finished, she dug up a French press from another cabinet. She had to clean it thoroughly; it had been so long since she'd had time to use the thing. She boiled water on the stove as she took a shower, finding that the workout from beating down the mushrooms combined with rifling through her kitchen and scrubbing the coffeepot had warmed her body enough that the cold water wasn't as terrible as it had been on the previous Tuesdays.

After she'd dried off, gotten dressed, and was drinking her hard-earned cup of extra-strong coffee, she got a text from Irene.

Where are you?? Everything okay?

Trina texted back, *I'm better than I was yesterday.*

Not sure what that means, but glad you're all right. You almost here?

I'll get there when I get there, she replied, adding a shrugging emoji for good measure. *I've got something to do first.*

And she picked up her skillet and headed over to Todd's apartment.

*   *   *

She was two hours late to work.

"Where have you been?" Irene ran up to her, looking pale. "Becky's been losing her shit, and it's kind of scary, even for her."

"Well, I had to take a second shower, and that one was warm so I didn't rush it," Trina explained. "Oh, and I had to find an umbrella."

"It's not raining today."

"I know." She held up her pocket umbrella with a little smile.

"Trina, I'm worried—"

"Katrina!"

She turned around to find Becky behind her, looking outraged. "Hey, Becks," she said. "How's it going?"

"Are you serious? You're, like, two hours late!"

Trina nodded. "I am."

A look of incredulity, a hand on a self-righteous hip. "Well, what do you have to say for yourself?"

"I have to say that I've been on time or early to this job every single day I've worked it, and the first thing I'd be asking an employee like me if she walked in two hours late would be if she was okay." She winked at Becky. "But I know watching out for other women isn't really your thing, so don't sweat it. It's not like any of us expect more from you."

Snorts and stifled laughs sounded from several nearby cubicles, and now Becky's face was all bewilderment as she looked around, suddenly aware that she might have wandered into enemy territory.

"Well, are you all right?"

"Hey, thanks for asking!" Trina replied brightly. "I had an issue with a man who's been stalking me and who broke into my apartment last night, but I think I've resolved it."

"Oh, my god," Irene gasped, putting a comforting hand on Trina's arm, and Becky took a step back, clearly not knowing what to do with all of these demonstrations of care and kindness among women.

"Okay," she said, practically pouting in her confusion, "I'm not sure how to mark that on your employee record. I'll just say you were sick this morning."

"Christ, Becky, are you one-hundred percent robot or just a cyborg?" Irene asked now, and the stifled laughter continued.

"Yo, Becks!" Kirk called from his cubicle, unaware of all that was transpiring. "You coming to hear about my crazy night or what?"

Becky huffed off in the direction of Kirk's cube, and there was some light, scattered applause.

"Are you really all right?" Irene asked Trina, and she realized that this coworker was probably a much better friend than the former college classmate she was scheduled to have dumplings with later. "Did you talk to the cops about this guy? You must have been terrified!"

"I took care of it," Trina said honestly. "Would you want to grab dinner after work tomorrow night?"

Irene smiled, then looked doubtful. "Mid-week dinner? I don't know, this place usually leaves me wiped."

"Well, the week is one day shorter, isn't it?"

"Yeah, that's true," Irene agreed. "Sounds great—thanks for the invite."

Trina nodded. It didn't matter that Wednesday wasn't likely to come anytime soon. When it finally did, she might have a friendship worth maintaining waiting for her.

"I'm going to run to the bathroom before I get started," she said.

Irene shook her head. "You're having quite the day, aren't you?"

Trina pretended to glance at the clock on the wall, but instead caught sight of Sean gently shaking a can of soda near the women's restroom.

She tucked the pocket-sized umbrella into her skirt's waistband and bloused her shirt down over it. "Yup, and it's not close to over yet."

*　　　*　　　*

When she got to the restaurant, she waited until she was sure Ginny was engrossed in flirting with Chet, then stealthily walked over to the old woman's table and slid into the seat opposite her.

"What, have I forgotten the existence of another one of my nieces?" the woman said by way of greeting. "Listen, sweetheart, if you're looking for cash, I'm fresh out."

"I promised you we'd have dinner together," Trina told the woman. "And I meant it."

"Oh, yeah? And when did this happen?"

"I can't exactly answer that," Trina said, "but I'm guessing you're short on company, given the week you've had?"

The woman stared at her for a long moment. "I'm Helen. If you're having dinner with a person, you should know her name at the very least."

"It's nice to meet you, Helen. I'm Trina."

Helen frowned. "That sounds like one of those hooker names. Are you trying to weasel money out of me later, after you butter me up with dumplings?"

"You know, I wish people would stop assuming I'm a prostitute," Trina said. "No offense to prostitutes."

"I would never set out to offend a woman of the night," Helen told her, one hand raised and the other over her heart. "But with a name like that, honey, what do you expect?"

"It's a nickname."

"For what?"

"Katrina."

Helen evaluated her, then nodded. "Well, that suits you better, after all. Trina it is."

Having earned permission to be called by her own name, Trina asked, "So, we're having the special?"

*   *   *

Helen was as fascinating as Trina had suspected she'd be, but it also turned out that the woman had spent a portion of her long life as a horticultural librarian. When Trina mentioned her mushroom conundrum in passing, Helen had offered a visit to her apartment.

"Now, don't judge," she said as she opened the door. "Would you believe I'm popular enough that I don't have time to stay home and clean regularly?"

"Yes," Trina told her honestly as she entered Helen's home.

The space was massive, as apartments went. The living room alone was larger than Trina's own studio, and it was filled from floor to ceiling with books. On the sides of shelves were framed Georgia O'Keeffe prints, and Trina saw that the two windows were home to sills full of intricate orchids.

"This wall here is devoted to botanical and horticultural materials," Helen told her, pointing to the longest wall of the living room and its seamless rows of shelves. "If you can't find what you're looking for there, you'll need to travel to an archive. I've done a damn good job of hoarding over the years, if I say so myself."

"And there are books about mushrooms here?"

Helen waved her over to one section of the towering wall of books. "Fungi weren't exactly my favorite topic, but there should be enough to help you find what you're looking for. Now, are you a tea or a coffee person at this hour?"

"Coffee at every hour."

Helen laughed as she headed towards her kitchen. "That's why we get along, you and I. Twin souls."

Trina began pulling books off the shelves and flipping through them, at random at first. Then, she started targeting those volumes that had pictures in them. She figured there was no way she'd be able to describe the mushrooms in a manner that they might be referred to within these books: "weird as fuck," "a pain in the ass," and "possibly immortal" did not seem like scientific terminology.

Finally, she found an image in one of the books that looked familiar. The caps and size seemed similar, but Trina was looking at a gigantic cluster where she had a comparatively small bunch on the pillar in her apartment.

"Although it's getting bigger by the day," she murmured as she began skimming the article.

Words began to pop out at her: *extremely rare; difficult to cultivate; poisonous.*

"Here's that coffee, as promised," Helen said, reemerging from her kitchen. "I put it on a proper tray and everything."

"Thanks, Helen." Trina turned around, smiling. "You have no idea how much I appreciate it."

Having set the tray on a low table, Helen settled into an armchair and gestured for Trina to take the loveseat across from her. "You find what you were looking for?"

She nodded as she sat down. "And I think I'm finally starting to understand this day."

"Well, when you figure it out completely, remember to explain it all to me, because I can't make fucking heads or tails of it."

*   *   *

Tuesday happened again. And again.

And again.

Trina didn't use a skillet every time she murdered Todd. She quickly learned that *amanita donummartis*, the mushroom that was growing in her apartment, could be boiled into tea, coffee—any hot drink, really. It seemed to taste all right, too, until it killed a person.

But Todd was the least of her problems. She couldn't quite convince herself not to go into work; that nagging thought that Wednesday might roll around eventually always stopped her from blowing off the office entirely.

She was having a little trouble keeping it together, though.

After two weeks of Sean and the inevitable warm soda, she'd tired of spare shirts, umbrellas, and rain slickers. She found herself getting a bit creative.

On one Tuesday, after he'd doused her, Trina had turned around and with a strength that surprised even her, she'd ripped his shirt right off of him. On another, she'd smuggled a warm bottle of champagne into the bathroom with her, shaken it the whole time she was peeing, and when she opened the door to a burst of soda, she immediately counter-attacked. The cork hit Sean right in the eye, knocking him flat on his ass, and there was much talk of workers' comp afterwards.

It was fun, Trina had to admit. But she was getting tired of being targeted every time she went to pee.

She decided to say as much on one particular Tuesday. Having opted to use her tried and true mini-umbrella when she'd left that morning (Sean hated it when she did this, which was an added bonus), Trina exited the bathroom unscathed.

"You know, you could've taken my eye out with that fucking thing!" he exclaimed, as he often did.

Trina shook her head. "That's the champagne cork," she assured him. "The umbrella only keeps my shirt safe, unfortunately."

"What are you talking about?"

"You need to stop with your bullshit, Sean," she told him.

"Hey, I was just trying to drink a soda. It's not my fault—"

"Every woman here, save for one very vapid office manager, will attest to the fact that you shook that can and waited for me to leave the bathroom," she said placidly. "Denying it just makes you look as immature and, well, lacking in several departments as the stunt itself does."

Irene passed by at that moment, mouthed *Yes!* and clapped her hands soundlessly together at Trina before walking back to her cube.

Sean caught the exchange, and his expression grew angry. "What's that supposed to mean?"

Trina shrugged. "You're clearly overcompensating for something. Most of us just aren't interested enough to wonder what it might be."

"You're such a fucking freak, Wells," he muttered as he started to walk away.

She stopped him, grabbing his arm hard.

"Hey!" His yelp was higher pitched than they both knew he'd wanted it to be.

"Don't worry," Trina told him, plastering an imitation of Becky's false smile onto her own face.

"Whether it's a cork, an umbrella, or something a bit more permanent: I promise I won't miss you next time."

She let him go and after a moment, heard him complaining to Kirk, "Can you believe that psycho?"

He really had no idea.

*   *   *

The goal was to start poisoning Kirk and Sean. She really couldn't just stop with Todd when the two of them were just as vile.

It was the principle of the thing.

But Trina's method of delivery was going to need some work, she realized. Todd would put anything she handed him in his mouth, but Kirk and Sean were strictly soda drinkers, never bothering with coffee or tea (the fucking monsters). And if Trina was going to get them to eat the mushrooms, she'd have to develop a skill that had evaded her up until that point in her life.

She needed to learn to bake.

Helen was more than willing to teach her the basics. Trina had started leaving the office a bit early—most Tuesdays, she was so erratic that Becky seemed too terrified to bother with her by end of day. If she got out quickly enough, she could catch Helen before she left for the restaurant.

It was always easy to strike up a friendship with the woman. They really were "twin souls," as Helen had said. Sometimes, Trina was a student looking for a specialist in botanical studies; sometimes, she was a prostitute who needed to learn about culinary plants for a particularly kinky client (Helen loved that introduction).

As they were baking and getting to know each other, Trina learned that Helen hadn't been kidding when she'd said she was low on cash.

"Well, this place is huge," Trina told her.

"Your point?"

She rolled her eyes. "Do you sleep in both bedrooms?"

"You mean a roommate?" Helen snorted. "I can't fucking stand most people, and the ones I could are all dropping around me like flies."

"Bingo, I remember," Trina murmured.

Helen eyed her warily. "I told you about that?"

Trina nodded, not specifying when.

The other woman shrugged. "I can't imagine living with anyone. You're the only person who's been in this apartment in years who I haven't wanted to throw right through the window."

Trina thought about that. "Well, I can't say I'm attached to my apartment."

"Are you serious?"

"I have a stalker," she said, which wasn't true at the moment but would be, come morning. "He lives on my floor."

"I don't envy you girls nowadays," Helen told her. "You put up with all the perverts and the bullshit we had to deal with, and they're slashing your benefits left and right."

"So, what do you think?"

"When is your current lease up?"

Trina almost said, *Whenever the fuck I want*, then realized the fearlessness that came with reliving a day dozens of times didn't necessarily translate to everyone who wasn't aware of reliving it with you. "Let's say...six weeks from now."

Helen nodded. "I can clean out the spare bedroom in that time. You don't have any pets, do you?"

"Just the mushrooms."

*   *   *

Her first office poisoning was more effective than she'd intended it to be. Kirk fell forward like a plank on a pirate ship, and Sean's eyes were wide and cold as they stared up at the ceiling, fishlike.

Becky's screams were so earsplitting, Trina decided she'd have to go, too. No one else in the office had started to scream.

After the cops had arrived to investigate, it hadn't been difficult for them to figure out the source of the poison. Trina was trying not to show her irritation with having to hang around the office. She was going to miss Helen at her apartment if this took much longer, and then she'd have to head to the restaurant. She hadn't brought enough brownies for Chet and Ginny, and she wasn't always able to avoid them when she got there. It took *forever* to get away from Ginny, and Trina and her soon-to-be roommate were supposed to watch a Parker Posey movie about librarians that night, although Helen didn't know that yet. They'd miss the whole first half if they got caught up at the dumpling place.

"And you, miss?" the detective was asking her. "You know anything about these brownies?"

He had a keen look in his eye, but Irene, who'd been standing next to Trina, snorted. "You're barking up the wrong tree there, officer," she said. "I've seen Trina try to microwave a cup of noodles and fuck it up."

"That so?"

Trina shrugged sheepishly. "What can I say? No one's taught me my way around a kitchen yet."

The detective stared at her a little longer, then moved on to another one of the women from their cubicle cluster. It made sense they were all being scrutinized, Trina figured. They all had reason to want to kill those two assholes.

She was just the one who'd decided to do it first.

*   *   *

That night, there was police tape blocking the entrance to her apartment building. Trina was surprised; once she'd stopped using the skillet, no one had thought to check on Todd at all. Then, beyond the tape in the lobby of her building, she recognized the detective who'd asked her about the brownies at the office earlier.

It would suck, Trina thought, if this was her final Tuesday. They'd no doubt searched her apartment and found the mushrooms by now. There would be no getting away with anything: Todd, Sean, Kirk, all of them would test positive for having *amanita donummartis* in their systems, and she would clearly be the one who had put it there.

And she hadn't even had the chance to kill Becky. Or Chet, for that matter.

Trina went over the numbers in her head. She'd gone through twenty-three Tuesdays so far, but she hadn't killed Todd until the fourth one. Technically, she'd committed over twenty murders, but she had only killed three people.

Would that get her a deal? She didn't think so.

But then, there was something about Tuesday: the happier she'd felt with each night that passed (or failed to); the friendships she'd forged that were better than the ones she'd shed; the fact that, once she'd stopped adhering to the original shitty script for the day, the mushrooms had come away from the pillar with just a gentle pinch of her fingers, ready to be added to whatever recipe she chose.

She had a kind of faith in this day, Trina realized. She was getting it more and more right with each Tuesday that passed (or didn't), but she hadn't perfected it yet. Once Becky and Chet were gone, she thought, maybe then she'd be able to move on to Wednesday. She would begin packing up her things, meet Helen and not be the only one to remember it, even start hanging out with Irene.

But first, she had to use this opportunity that was being gifted to her to understand how she'd fucked up and gotten the cops on her case. They would have her for interrogations until midnight; she was reasonably confident she could get them to tip their hand by then, show her what mistakes she'd made.

With a wide smile on her face that had never existed before Tuesday, Trina made for the lobby.

The Family Wolves

Rose petals filled my head, swirling with a gust raised by a memory that was not my own. And then I felt cool, dry lips on my forehead and knew she'd come home.

"I wasn't asleep," I told my mother.

She almost smiled, which was her smile. "Then I can't be blamed for waking you."

I struggled to push myself up, the flu weakening even the sinewy strength of my hands. She made a gesture to stop me.

"I just came in. I haven't had a chance to warm the soup yet."

"Can I help?"

Another near-smile. "You can stay right here. It'll be ready before I catch you not sleeping again."

I gave in, my body exhausted from fever and dehydration. When I awoke once more, there was a steaming bowl in front of my face. The herbs mixed into the broth were strong, and I found my eyes watering.

"One spoon at a time," she instructed, seeming to sense how overwhelmed I was. "You'll polish it off before you know it."

"Is this what your mother used to make?"

The question brought a cloud into those eyes that were nearly identical to mine, so much so that even as a child, I could see my own resemblance to her. It was stronger than both of my sisters', one of whom was a dead ringer for our aunt, and the other who we'd been told looked like our father, though we couldn't quite see it yet.

"Yes, I believe it was."

"But you're not sure?"

The guilt rose in me even amidst the fever as I asked the question, because I knew that pressing the subject made things hard for her. But even now, as she performed this act of caregiving and love, I couldn't help but demand to know about my grandmother. She had died when my mother was young; how she had died, neither I nor my sisters had been able to ascertain.

"The broth smells just like the one she used to make when I was sick," she said. "So, I must be getting the herbs right."

I didn't know what to ask next, so I finished the soup and went back to sleep. My sisters were away with our aunt; once it was clear I had a bad flu, rather than risk the household, my mother had suggested they spend the weekend enjoying the last of the warm weather by the seaside while I rested up and got well again.

The crush of roses seemed to take me in once more, though I would not remember them by the time the fever broke. And I would not know their meaning until she finally told me, which would not be until I was nearly a grown woman. But this was one of few times I had my mother to myself, and so I clutched onto the rarity and cherished it.

*   *   *

I knew we were different from other families the year my aunt became briefly possessed, and my sisters and I had to take part in the ritual that freed her. I'd known ritual before, but thought I experienced it as any child does: planting flowers in our garden in the spring, lighting candles in windows in the winter, kisses before bed, coffee at breakfast, chanting at midnight beneath every full moon, leaving food for the fairies on solstice nights, reading cards and runestones for company whenever some might stop by. It was all the same in my eyes until that malevolent spirit was driven out by a circle of powerful women, our beautiful mother at the helm and us girls looking on in breathless, heart-racing anticipation of our fate. That was when I realized that there was something special about us, something that did not apply in other households.

Wynna, my older sister, was twelve at the time. I'd been born just behind her and had recently turned eleven, and Jenny was nine. She had the smallest part to play in the whole thing, being still so young, but that was another strange thing about the girls in our family: we didn't always get to count on being young, as I would come to learn.

If you've ever seen a spirit possession, you know how hideous it can be. It is that much worse in a woman who is also a witch; the thing inside will gain strength from her powers, use them to its own ends. And, according to our aunt in her account of things afterwards, being unable to speak one's own mind or move where one wishes was nothing compared to losing one's magic.

"Something's wrong with Auntie Jay," Jenny had said on a cold morning as Wynna and I set the table.

She was speaking of her namesake, but everyone called my mother's younger sister Jennifer "Jay." I had asked her once why she used the nickname, as I envied my own little sister her name. I found Jennifer much more beautiful than Susan, my own appellative.

"Oh, I think someone called me jaybird, a long time ago," she'd giggled, wrinkling her nose. She had a girlish aspect about her, even years later when her hair had turned silver and her knuckles knotted with age. "I guess it stuck from that point on, because I've never managed to get rid of it."

"Was it Grandpa?" I'd asked, thinking that was the name a father might use. I didn't remember my own father and had no point of reference but girlish, wishful fantasy.

Aunt Jay's face had grown dark. "I told you, I don't remember where it came from," she'd said, her voice turning uncharacteristically cold. "Don't ask me about it again."

After my initial hurt, I hadn't thought much about that exchange. But now, the fearful note in Jenny's voice brought the memory back to me, and I prepared to ask her to tell us more. Wynna beat me to the punch.

"What are you talking about, Jenny?" she asked, frowning. Wynna had grown into her role as big sister quite determinedly, if her application of her duties was a touch uneven; when she wasn't bossing us, she was doting on us.

Jenny shrugged in the way of young children.

"Speak up," Wynna instructed, but at that moment, our aunt came skipping down the stairs and Jenny stayed quiet.

"Good morning, girls!" Jay said brightly.

There was a heavy pause, and then Wynna, taking charge as she always did, smiled back at our aunt. "Morning, Aunt Jay. Are you having coffee?"

"You know, I just might." Aunt Jay winked at her. "Leave a mug by my place setting, just in case?"

Nothing seemed amiss, but I could see Jenny's small frame shrinking into itself. I resolved to remain watchful.

Later that day, I started towards the sun room and heard a shrill sound. Instinct told me to approach in silence, and so I slid my shoes off and tiptoed over.

Jay was standing there, a bird struggling in her left hand which was locked around it like iron. With her right hand, she was yanking feathers from the creature, blood coming away with some of them, the bird obviously in pain.

The breath of "Stop!" that escaped my lips came without my consent, but I was glad for it. Her eyes shifted to where I stood, her grip loosened, and despite the loss of many feathers, the desperate creature managed to get away through an open window.

Aunt Jay smiled at me with all of her teeth, and in a stroke of luck, my mother walked in the front door right at that moment.

I ran straight upstairs to my sisters first, not thinking my mother might be the one to speak to. "Jenny's right," I announced on finding them grinding herbs in the attic, pestles churning steadily until I burst in, breathless. "Something's wrong with Aunt Jay."

It was Wynna who told our mother what I'd seen, but she came up to speak with me. I had refused to leave my room and go down to dinner that night.

"Susan?" my mother asked gently as she pushed open the door.

I couldn't help it; the moment I saw her, I was in tears.

"Wynna told me," she said. "And I saw for myself. Don't worry, love. I'm going to fix it."

"How?" I wanted to know. "If Aunt Jay is...wrong, or whatever. How can you fix it?"

"What you saw was not your aunt," she told me firmly.

"I don't understand."

My mother sighed, hesitant. "There are people who go bad; there are some who are born bad. And then there are things that overtake people, keep them quiet while they use their skin, their faces, to do bad things."

"How can you tell the difference?" I wanted to know.

Her near-smile. "I know my sister, as you know both of yours. The thing inside of Jay is dark and clever, but I can see it wearing her."

I nodded, taking this in. "So, how are you going to take care of it?"

"With help from others, including you, if you're willing. Do you want to help free your aunt?"

I could only nod again, but felt far from the comfort my mother was offering.

*   *   *

The thing inside our aunt was hideous, and we came to know it soon enough. It contorted her body, twisted her face, but worst of all, it spoke to us in her voice. The sweet tones I'd grown up trusting spoke of vile things, many of which I had not learned of yet.

Wynna would pull me and Jenny away when the talk went in that direction, but as our mother gathered a coven and the women arrived in a trickle, Aunt Jay's condition worsened.

"Why can't they all get here faster?" Wynna asked in frustration one evening, hearing the rattling screams and moans coming from Aunt Jay's room. "Don't they realize how serious this is?"

"You must have patience, love," our mother said, moving to smooth my older sister's hair. "They are making their way."

But Wynna's disposition was turning from independent and willful to downright belligerent. She jerked her head away from our mother's touch. "I don't understand how a person can't show up in a crisis."

"Women in this family are always in crisis, Wynna." Now our mother's voice was harder, and I saw for the first time how she and Wynna would come to butt heads in the years to come. "I suggest you get used to it."

One of the visitors was named Candace, a wispy woman with wispier hair and a breathy voice, and she chose that moment to come into the kitchen. "Is it too late for me to brew a pot of tea?"

It wasn't the first time Candace had interrupted a tense moment. She also had a way with Jenny that seemed to have reassured my sister for the first time since the malevolent spirit had made its presence within our aunt known.

"Of course not, Candace," my mother said, wrapping a shawl around her shoulders. "Wynna will help you find what you need."

"Where are you going?" I asked. It was always frightening when the house had Aunt Jay in it and not our mother.

Her eyes softened as they settled on me. "Just to the greenhouse. There are things we'll need in the days to come, and it's high time I go and begin gathering them."

Candace smiled in my direction. "Maybe you can help Wynna set me up with the tea, Susan. Seems like it could be a three-person job."

After our mother had gone and we'd brewed the tea, Candace sat with us at the table and we drank in silence until Wynna slammed her cup down in frustration. "What does that even mean, our family's always in crisis?"

Jenny and I had jumped at the outburst, but Candace kept drinking from her cup, seemingly unbothered. "I would guess your mother's trying to keep you from making any of the mistakes she's fallen into," she offered gently.

"I don't know how," Wynna snapped. "She's cryptic, and she's inviting cryptic people in."

Candace surprised me by giggling, and then Wynna by suddenly laughing with her. "Oh, I'm sorry, my dear," the woman said, shaking her head. "You're not the first to accuse me of being a bit vague, and you won't be the last. But then, when you see things as I do, you get used to the vague."

"And you don't want to try to be a little more clear?" The request came sincerely now from my older sister, more pleading than challenging.

Candace nodded. "I'll say this, girls: every family has its wolves, the things it carries with which it must grapple. And in your mother's case, I think that whatever wolves she's seen in the past are still snapping at the door, at least in her mind."

We were silent for a long moment. For whatever reason, the image of rose petals raining down on a white tile floor filled my mind, and I found that I could almost smell them as I sat there, gazing down into my teacup. The scent was overpowering, and I fought the urge to gag.

"That's not clearer at all," Jenny suddenly said, breaking the silence with wide eyes, and now I joined Wynna and Candace in their laughter. It proved infectious, and by the time my mother came back, all our eyes were teary and our sides ached.

"Should I be worried about more possessing spirits in my house?" she asked, though I could tell she was pleased.

"Not at all, Diana," Candace assured her. "The only spirit I've found within these girls is a charm they've inherited from the women who raised them. What a beautiful home this is!"

And, I reflected for the first time in my eleven years, it was.

*   *   *

It had always been complicated, bringing other children into our home. We were hardly the only witches in the region; not even the only ones in town, though the other family lived a good distance away and we didn't socialize with them much.

But when Wynna, Jenny, and I had friends over, there was always an inevitable moment when we were made to defend ourselves, to explain how we lived or even our home itself. I didn't realize until I was much older that this was not the case in every house. I'd given my young playmates the benefit of the doubt, had figured I, too, would have questions about what was strange if I had gone over to their homes. And it was not until I was thirteen, preparing to meet friends and attend the end-of-year school dance, that I would think to ask my mother, "Why did we only ever have friends come over the house?"

She tilted her head as she continued last-minute adjustments to the hem of my dress, clearly confused by the question. Aunt Jay, sitting by and arranging the flowers that would go in my hair, chuckled a little and voiced the confusion she and my mother shared. "You didn't like having friends over, Susan?"

I shook my head. "No, I mean: why didn't I ever go to anyone else's house to play?"

They shared a dark look, and not for the first time, I wondered what it was that my mother and her sister recalled that I could not remember, if it was a thing I'd been around to remember at all. Was it something from their girlhood or from mine? And why did I feel a hopeless cold whenever I realized I'd stumbled onto it once more, never intending to but always wanting to know what the thing was?

"These should look perfect with that dress," Aunt Jay told me, standing to bring over the bright yellow flowers she'd woven together for my hair.

"I would have preferred roses," I said sullenly, and my mother let out a sound that was strange and breathless, something between a gargle and a hiss. Then she stood and walked briskly from the room.

I regretted the words instantly. It was as though I had known exactly what to say to push my mother to a limit, a wall I had been staring at for years and years but could not peer over to understand what lay beyond.

Aunt Jay looked down and I saw a tremble in her hands.

"I didn't mean that," I started to backtrack, then decided that it was time to push my aunt, as well. "But I'm not a baby anymore, Aunt Jay. I know there's something you've both been keeping from me, and I can handle it. I wish one of you would just tell me."

Now my aunt clicked her tongue and began to arrange the flowers in my hair. "No one thinks you're a baby, Susan. But you're mistaken in believing that it's you who can't handle what drove your mother from this room." She handed me a mirror. "Hold this high for me, love, so I can see the front of your head while I weave this bit in."

It was the end of the matter for that day, but I learned a great lesson: that even though so much of what my mother and aunt did was to protect us, to keep us safe and raise us well, they also could fear for themselves. It was something that had not occurred to me, especially because of Aunt Jay's possession. Watching both of those women brave the expulsion of that malevolent spirit had convinced me that they were as invincible a force as I would ever meet, and that once I was a woman, I would become such a force, too. I didn't see that raw and aching side both hid away from us, didn't think it was possible for such strength to harbor such vulnerability.

I knew then that I still had much to learn in the years ahead.

*   *   *

Candace was a comforting presence in contrast to the spirit wearing our aunt. Where the house had taken on a chill, she was a spot of brightness, and one night,

Jenny and I found her out in front of the greenhouse, casting.

"Hey, Candace," I greeted her, not wanting to startle her with our approach as her eyes were shut.

At the sound of my voice, her eyelids flew open. Jenny and I froze in our tracks: Candace's gentle brown eyes had been set alight, glowing in the dark like some fairy from a faraway wood. She raised one finger to her lips, then shut her eyes once more and commenced chanting.

We waited. Finally, she thrust her hands like knives into the soil on either side of her, and I felt a pulse through my feet. I looked at my sister, whose wide eyes confirmed she had felt it, too.

"I apologize for making you wait, girls," Candace said, and her eyes were back to their familiar, everyday state.

"What were you doing?" I asked in awe. I had seen my mother and my aunt cast from time to time, but they mostly did simple things: sealing up a leak, helping loaves of bread to rise, steadying the flickering of our electricity during a storm. Never had I felt anything like the magic Candace had been engaging.

"Well, I noticed that the creature inhabiting your aunt was extending its reach in this direction. I wanted to make sure to stop its influence before it got into the greenhouse and wrecked our supplies."

"How could you tell?" Jenny wanted to know.

Candace pointed to the ground. We had to squint, with the moon mostly hidden behind clouds, but then I caught sight of an almost claw-like pattern of grooves in the ground. They were indeed extending from our house towards the greenhouse.

"It's not unusual for such a thing to sabotage those trying to remove it," she went on. "I had an idea it might try something like this, so I knew to look for the signs. You both will learn, eventually."

As the three of us walked back towards the house together, Jenny said to Candace, "I wish you could stay afterwards. I like having you here."

"That's the sweetest thing you could have said." Candace offered my sister a broad smile, and I realized there was something impish about her, something ever-youthful and charming that had always been there but that I had overlooked. I felt silly for not noticing her resemblance to a fairy until her eyes had lit up the night. "What if I promise it won't be my last visit?"

"Can you?" Jenny pleaded.

Candace nodded. "I knew your mother and aunt when we were all girls like you, and I'm sorry that life has kept us apart for so many years. We'll make it a point to stay in touch more."

Our mother was waiting by the kitchen door. "Everything all right?"

"Susan and Jenny were just helping me clean up a mess your uninvited guest had been making," Candace reassured her. "The greenhouse is well-guarded. We'll have everything we need tomorrow."

"What's tomorrow?" I asked.

"Tomorrow, our final guests arrive," my mother told me. "And we get your aunt back."

Later that night, Jenny whispered to me in the dark of Wynna's room. We'd been camping out in there since Aunt Jay had been overtaken by the possessing spirit.

"Do you think the wolves are inside of Auntie Jay?"

"What do you mean?" I asked her, half-asleep already.

"The claw marks in the ground: do you think those are the wolves Candace told us about?"

I thought on this, and as it often did when things around me inexplicably turned towards a heaviness, a darkness that I could not quite discern, my mind drew up the smell of roses and a deep sense of dread.

"No," I told Jenny. "I think she meant something else."

*   *   *

Jenny would have struggles in the coming years, things that Wynna and I would never go through.

I was studying late one night. It was my junior year, and I was trying to keep my grades up while looking at colleges—all local, as Wynna had gone far away and I felt it necessary to stay near my family, although Aunt Jay had basically trailed Wynna to school. She went to visit her almost as often as she was home. Wynna would never admit as much, but I knew the fact that she kept allowing our aunt to visit meant she missed home.

Suddenly, in the midst of a particularly difficult page of trigonometry, I heard the sounds of glass breaking. I stood up and looked out the window, finding movement in the greenhouse.

My mother had gone to the store a little earlier, realizing she'd run out of sugar and determined to get her baking done that night and not the next day. I knew I was alone and would have to deal with this myself.

I whispered a protective spell, sealing it by slipping into my pocket a gold coin and a bit of dried thyme from the small store of materials I kept in my room. I felt the spell settle on me like a weighted cloak, then went downstairs and grabbed my mother's rolling pin for good measure. The glass continued to shatter as I made for the greenhouse.

When I got closer, I realized the shape within was my sister's silhouette. I pulled open the door. "Jenny, what the hell?"

She swayed as she turned towards me, and I saw a look of confused anger on her tear-stained face. She stank of alcohol.

"You're drunk?" I demanded.

"Looks like it," she said, punctuating the thought with a hiccup-burp.

"You're fourteen!" I was aghast at the state of her. Wynna had been downright mean through long stretches of high school, and I was something of a nervous wreck, but neither of us had ever gotten like this.

"And still drunk, somehow."

I put my hands on my hips. "Jenny, what are you doing? Why are you shattering the herbs?"

"Do you know what the boys in my grade want from girls?" she asked me.

I could guess. "Why does that matter?" I asked her, trying to ease her out of her belligerent state. "You don't need them. You have us."

She laughed bitterly. "Yup," she agreed. "I have this family, this house where no one is normal and no one will say why."

"Well, I doubt the boys at school don't know we're witches by now."

Jenny shook her head. "No, it's not *that*. It's not that. It's what they learned about us, about the women who live here. It's what their fathers and their grandfathers tell them about us."

"Jenny—"

"The boys in my grade," she said, swaying and hiccupping more, "want what they can have. They want pretty, they want sweet, and they want something to take their bad feelings out on."

"That's not you," I told her sternly.

"Oh, it is!" she told me. "I heard it from Jake. We come from a family of sluts—did you know that? Diana and Jennifer, power and magic notwithstanding, both slept around all through high school, and then our mother ended up with 'the kind of man a slut deserves.'" She punctuated these last words with air quotes, letting me know they weren't hers.

"Jake's been a shit for a long time, Jenny. You shouldn't listen to him."

"And if I," she continued, "if I expect to be treated differently, well, I'd better think again. I'm not pretty or sweet enough, but I can take it, apparently." She looked around the greenhouse, anger again filling her eyes. Spying a jar of lavender, she held it high above her head, then let it fall to the ground and shatter with the other jars she'd broken.

"Jenny, come back in the house," I said quietly. "We'll talk inside."

"I hate that house. I hate what happened in this family, what no one has ever told us happened but that you and I know happened."

"What?" I whispered.

But she suddenly started puking, and I was able to hold her while she was sick and then coax her back to the kitchen where I made her tea. I didn't even think as I prepared the blend, my focus on how worried I was for my little sister.

As I set the tea on the table, she breathed in the steam, then looked up at me with tired eyes. "See? You know. You've known all along, and now I know, too."

I put the rose hips back in the cupboard and left to go clean up her mess in the greenhouse, saying nothing as I did.

*   *   *

The morning after Candace worked her magic outside of the greenhouse, there were twenty women gathered including my mother. Two had arrived during the night. And although the house was full, it was quiet, bearing the sort of tense silence that indicates waiting for something.

I remembered a gathering like this, though I could not pinpoint when it had taken place and was still too sleepy to think on it. I was helping my mother set the breakfast plates, and we were at opposite ends of the long dining table that could seat the full house of women and then some.

"This house hasn't had so many witches in it for a very long time," my mother said to me, her voice warm and reassuring as though my aunt's skin being worn by a malevolent being was nothing to fret over.

Still not fully awake, I nodded, yawning. "Not since Grandma died."

A handful of forks slid from my mother's hand and clattered all over the floor, and sleepiness left me immediately. She was suddenly drawn, staring at me with hollow eyes that held fear and something else in them.

"That's all right, now." Candace's warm voice entered the room, breaking the silent moment between us. "Susan, why don't you go help Jenny with the teas and coffees for everyone?"

Another woman who'd arrived the day before, Phyllis, was already by my mother's side, rubbing her back and murmuring soothing words. Candace gave me a smile, kind but forceful, letting me know I was to leave the room.

"She—she knew," my mother was saying to Phyllis, shaking her head and still staring at me like I was a strange animal, an aberration of some kind.

"It's not the girl's fault she can see so clearly," Phyllis told her, clicking her tongue as I left the room. "You think that's a wall around your heart, Diana, but to your daughter, it's merely a veil waiting to be lifted."

"And when the time is right," I heard Candace interject, "Susan will see what she needs to. But for today, our focus will remain on why we've all gathered. We must think of Jay and nothing else."

"Of course," I could hear my mother murmuring. "I know you're both right. I'll be fine, I just…I need all of this to be over with."

"What happened?" Jenny asked me.

I shook my head. I didn't know.

*   *   *

Wynna was upstairs in her room, reading the cards. I stood and watched her from the doorway for a bit. She would do a three-card spread, frown, then throw the cards into the deck once more, shuffle and repeat the whole process.

"Not liking what you see?" I asked.

"It doesn't make sense," she told me.

"Are you drawing for Auntie Jay?" I was worried; if Wynna didn't like what she was seeing, did that mean we would fail in driving out the malevolent spirit?

She shook her head. "It's not just that. I'm trying to make sense of something I'm seeing, something more long-term."

"Show me," I said, sitting on the bed with her.

She laid out the cards once more. "See, here—this seems to suggest we'll be successful at getting rid of the possession."

"Well, then that's good, isn't it?"

Wynna pointed to the third card. "But in this position, this means that there is unrest down the line of our family. We won't have gotten rid of it once the spirit's gone."

"I don't understand."

"Neither do I," she told me. "If the thing wearing Aunt Jay isn't what's threatening us, then what is?"

She shuffled, drew once more.

The cards were the same.

"Girls," Candace appeared at the door, glancing at the cards between us, "there's no time to deal with the future now. The present is waiting; come help us with your aunt."

*   *   *

My mother was sitting in the kitchen late one night, staring into a cup of tea.

"Did you see the mail?" I asked her.

She looked up at me with happiness in her eyes. "I did. Jenny's top choice of school, and the envelope is big."

I shook my head. "Overseas! And I thought Wynna had gone far away."

"Jenny has always wanted to leave, deep down." She stirred her tea. "And she deserves that much."

I sat at the table across from her. "You've never spoken to me about any of it."

She tensed, as she always did when I got close to the topic, but I was a young woman now and didn't scare the way I did as a girl. I reached forward and took her hand.

"I know. I know Grandpa killed her."

There was a long, quiet pause between us. Then she drew in a breath and began to speak to me. "Jay wasn't in the apartment at the time. I'm grateful to this day that she wasn't. It was just me and your grandmother, preparing dinner together. I was six years old, and she was teaching me to hold a knife without hurting myself so I could help cut the vegetables.

"He came in drunk. I don't remember him well, but what I do recall is constantly being afraid and the overbearing smell of spirits. It's why we've never kept any in the house; I can't stand that smell."

I thought of roses and how I avoided that scent myself, but I said nothing, afraid she would stop speaking again.

"His eyes finally settled on the knife in my hands. He asked her what kind of a mother gave a child a knife?" Tears filled her eyes. "I remember thinking when I was a little older, if only I'd learned to use that knife sooner, maybe I could have stopped him."

"You were only six," I reminded her. "And he was a big man, wasn't he?"

She tilted her head at me. "Not so big as all that, though he seemed a mammoth to me at the time. From photographs, much later on, I would realize he was actually rather short. But she was frail, and in that moment she didn't even manage to get the protective spell out before he'd hit her in the mouth so hard she couldn't speak. Then, his hands were around her throat." She stopped, looking down at the tea.

"And the roses?" I asked.

My mother's eyes settled on me, the haunted look she'd worn now evolving into something more quietly disturbed. "My love, there were no roses. Not...not that night."

I was confused. "But I always smell them," I said. "And I know that's tied to what you haven't been telling me."

New tears fell. "This is so hard, Susan."

"I know," I told her. I didn't know, not exactly, but I was trying to understand, for love of her. "Please tell me the rest."

"The roses," she finally said, "were from your father."

That made no sense to me. "But Dad was kind. I remember, he was...gentle, even. And he couldn't have hurt anyone, he was so sick from the cancer treatments..."

"Jenny's father died of cancer," she whispered. "He was a good, kind man, as you say, and one of the first things he did when we were married was formally adopt my two daughters from a previous marriage, both of whom he loved as his own."

Now my world began to spin.

"What happened to—who was our father?" I managed, barely. "Mine and Wynna's?"

"A man like my own father, though I didn't see it until I was too close."

"Is he dead, too?"

I didn't know why that was the first thing I asked. My mother wasn't old, and unless there had been a large age difference between them, there was no reason to think that he'd have also experienced the untimely death that the man I'd always believed to be my father had suffered. Perhaps I wanted him dead, with the knowledge I now had of what he'd done.

"He's dead to me, but as far as I know, he hasn't passed." She sighed. "The night that you've glimpsed was the night Jay came to bring me home. He'd bought roses to make up for how badly he'd hurt me the day before, as he did so often. Add their perfume to the list of scents your mother cannot abide."

"And he—your first husband—he was a big man?"

"Yes," she told me. "And that night, apology bouquet be damned, he was angry again. If Jay hadn't shown up, you and I would not have made it."

"I was there?"

"Not yet. I was about six months pregnant with you."

"And Wynna?"

"Asleep in bed through the whole thing, as far as I knew. Wynna could always sleep through anything."

"With nightmares," I reminded her. "Wynna's always had horrific nightmares."

We were silent for a long time.

"Will you tell your sisters?" she finally asked.

I hadn't even begun to think about that. I was still reeling from all I'd heard. "Only if it will help them to know," I said. "Maybe Wynna could benefit, but Jenny's finally moved past so much. I don't want to drag her back down to where she was a year ago."

She nodded, then said, "There may come a time when they both need to know." I saw a look in her eye I recognized. I'd caught it in the mirror when I'd known things that had not yet come to pass, something that happened to me more and more as I aged.

"Candace is coming back soon for her yearly visit, isn't she?" I asked. I knew the answer, but I wanted to give my mother an escape from the conversation.

"She is." My mother gave that near-smile, and said, "I am so very proud of you, Susan. You and your sisters make me feel I did the right thing all those years ago."

"The right thing?"

She gestured around us. "Buying this house with Jay and giving you a place to live. Not running from the town where we lost our mother, where I almost lost myself."

"You didn't want a fresh start?"

"You don't get a fresh start when you run from something dark, my love. It follows you until you face it. By making a home here, I was given..." Her eyes searched the darkness outside, and I realized I could hear the chimes just beyond the kitchen windows singing on a gentle night breeze. "A reckoning."

Now, I smiled. "The women in this family always find trouble, don't we?"

"But we always get each other out of it."

*   *   *

We had to drag Aunt Jay out into the night, shrieking and cursing beneath a full and shining moon.

We might have worried that she would rouse the neighbors, but I didn't think anyone who heard the sounds she was making would want to draw closer to the source. Besides, our town knew better than to enter into the affairs of witches when the moon was full and midnight near.

The ground beneath her cracked and buckled with the force of the spirit wearing her skin, its rage formidable against the gathered coven of women intending to send it from the powerful shell it had claimed as its new home.

It threatened us all intermittently; some of the women blushed as secrets and thoughts they'd kept hidden were shrieked into their faces, easily gleaned by this horror within my aunt. When it turned her eyes on me and Wynna, holding hands to one side, it grinned wolfishly and sang, "Poor little witches, not a chance in hell you'll stray from that path your mothers have set you on. And what of the youngest? She'll suffer the most of all of you the minute she cracks her lips."

My mother slapped Aunt Jay's face, startling me and Wynna even more than the malevolent spirit had frightened us.

"Don't listen to these antics, my loves," she told us in a firm voice. "A creature will say anything when it knows it's about to go to slaughter. Why don't you go over by Candace?"

My mother was at the head of the circle formed, Candace her counterpart at its base. She let Wynna and I stand on either side of her, and I found that the woman on my left was none other than Phyllis, who'd spoken to my mother about me that morning.

"You all right, Susan?" she asked.

I nodded mutely. I wasn't, exactly; the thing's threat against Jenny wasn't entirely lost on me. I didn't understand its more filthy suggestions, but the malintent hadn't missed me, and given what Wynna had drawn from the deck, I was more uncertain about our futures than ever.

"Do you know what flower you're named for, my girl?" Phyllis asked, beginning to bundle the herbs set before her in the circle as all the witches around us were doing. I started to follow suit.

"No," I replied. "I didn't even know I was named after a flower."

"Oh, yes," she told me. "The Black-Eyed Susan, that yellow flower you're adding to your bundle just now."

I looked down and saw what I'd assumed to be a peculiar kind of yellow daisy in my hands.

"It's a sweet little flower, underestimated by many," she continued. "But don't doubt a Black-Eyed Susan can pack a punch."

"What are its properties?" I wanted to know.

"Healing and cleansing, mainly."

I shrugged. "That's not so different from these others in the bundle."

"You're not wrong, but for the way it heals. If you're ever leaching poison, you'll want some in your pantry."

I rolled my eyes. "How often do you have to get rid of poison?"

Phyllis gave me a steady look. "We're working on getting it from your aunt now, ain't we?"

I realized I'd spoken foolishly, and kept binding the plants together. By the time I'd finished, my mother had already set her own bundle alight with a whispered spell and a wave of her hand. She turned to the women on either side of her, offered the flame, and they passed it around the circle in turn. Phyllis held her bundle out and mine ignited; Wynna and I lit Candace's together, and the circle was cast.

*   *   *

Wynna went first, though I was the one who worked the spell to open the front door.

"Jen?"

Our sister was sitting on the floor in front of a worn-out sofa, her expression dazed. To her left was an open bottle of vodka, two-thirds drunk. One of her socks was halfway off her foot, making her seem vulnerable as she had when we were small children and she looked up to me.

I hoped in that moment I still had some sway over her, some influence that would get her out of this.

"Jenny," Wynna said, and though she had always been the strongest of us three, her voice broke on our sister's name.

Jenny's eyes dragged from the floor to us, and as we came into focus, she smiled wryly. "Look who's here. I must be in worse shape than I thought."

We sat on the floor with her. "What's going on, Jen?" I asked.

She shook her head. "It's nothing. I just had a rough day at work. It's really nothing."

"It's not nothing," Wynna said, the firmness of her voice returning to her. "We haven't heard from you in three months, Jenny. And Susan and I both know something's wrong."

"You shouldn't have come," she told us. "I'm really fine. We're fine."

"Where's Beth?" Wynna asked.

"She went...she's with a friend. For work, I mean. They're having dinner."

My eyes had begun to drift around the apartment, and I started to see traces of things that had happened there. Screaming in front of the mirror that hung by the door. Weeping on the sofa. A strike across the face and searing pain in its wake, just in front of the stove.

"Oh, Jenny," I sighed. "You don't have to lie to us."

"I'm not—"

"When did she start hitting you?"

I'd stopped avoiding difficult things from that night when my mother and I had spoken. I'd learned there was too much at stake to remain silent, and that people kept quiet about exactly the things they shouldn't, especially in our family.

My words brought tears to Jenny's eyes, and she shook her head in protest. "No, it's—she doesn't mean anything. I can handle—really, I'm handling it."

Wynna said, "You're coming home with us."

"No!" she shouted. "No, I'm fine here. I'm fine."

"The hell you are. Susan, get her things packed."

"Wynna, just wait," I said, putting a steadying hand on my older sister's arm. She was twenty-eight years old, more forceful and beautiful than ever, and I had not yet figured out how to talk with her about our family's past, though it had been years since my mother and I had spoken. And, I realized, she wasn't the sister who needed to hear it. Not on this night, and not in this moment.

"Jenny," I said gently, and I put an arm around her. She stank of vodka and puke, which I knew was a good thing; it meant that, although she was drunk, she wasn't as drunk as she must have been before we got there.

"I'm fine," she murmured, but allowed me to pull her into a hug.

"Do you remember," I began, stroking her hair, "when you asked me if the wolves were in Aunt Jay? Do you remember that?"

After a quiet moment, she sniffled. "Yeah."

"Well, they're not. They're in us."

"Who?"

"All of us, but right now, you. This," I grabbed the bottle, held it in my hand, "this is one of them. And what Beth did to you that night in front of the stove? That's another."

I looked up at Wynna, who seemed confused but willing to let me do whatever it was I was doing.

"And the fact that it took us so long to come together again," I continued, "that's a big one. But we are going to fix that, right now."

I went into the kitchen and dug in the cabinets until I found salt and a jar of star anise. I poured water into a shallow bowl, and sat with my sisters once again.

I began marking the circle in salt, and Wynna helped me. We set the bowl of water in the middle and each took a palmful of anise, even Jenny, reluctant though her movements were.

"Now what?" she asked sulkily, but when she met my eyes, she did give a little smile.

"Good question," Wynna said, looking to me.

"Now, we do something we learned to years ago," I told them. "We drive away the unwanted thing. After all, if it comes down to betting between witches and wolves, my money isn't on the wolves."

Together, as sisters, we began to cast.

*   *   *

Plumes of smoke surrounded us, creating a veritable dome above the circle, and I felt the power of all the women around me take root, dive down into the earth so that the thing within my aunt could not burrow or fly away.

It screamed and threatened in words I could not begin to understand. The sight of Wynna on the other side of Candace offered me some small comfort, her face reflecting the fear I felt. We locked eyes for a moment, and a ludicrous smile, evidence of a shared thrill and horror, passed between us. It was the first time I could remember being actively grateful to have sisters, to have someone before and after me with whom I could share anything and everything.

I saw then that Jenny was standing beyond Wynna, watching the ritual with a look on her face I didn't understand. I could not get her to meet my eyes the way Wynna had; to this day, I wonder whether we would have had to go into that apartment and heal her in a circle cast in salt with herbs like stars in the palms of our hands, if only she could have caught my gaze that day.

But all of a sudden, Aunt Jay gave a sound like metal shredding itself, and I saw the thing leave her, much as any animal sheds unwanted skin. It was before her, and she stood, beautiful and powerful as our mother, who moved to allow a place for her in the circle.

Now one of those gathered to battle the spirit that had been within her, Jay's face took on a stark fierceness. Eventually, I would come to realize it didn't matter that we were not impervious as witches. Whether we could falter or be harmed was not the important thing. What was important was that, should anything try to hurt one of us, there would be others waiting to help reckon with it, exorcise it, burn it away and make it regret it had trifled with a witch in the first place.

And beneath smoke and a moon heavy with witching power, that was exactly what we did.

And This, Her Art

It was cold behind the restaurant, and the dumpster reeked of water stagnant with rot.

I had been waiting three hours, as it was. What was another, or another beyond that? Night stretched behind me as it did ahead; for all I knew, this cool darkness would be my life for years to come.

Not for the first time, my mind entertained the idea that she was a shadow of me and nothing tangible, nothing I could kiss or crush. You can't make love to an echo of yourself any more than you can worship at her feet.

But there had been something convincing about our last conversation. I didn't think I could have explained the exhibition the way she had, given the artworks on display and the narrative texture that spilled from her lips, painted neon orange for that night.

The neon sign above me flickered for the three-hundredth time. I blew vapor from my own dry mouth, no paint or polish to tint that breath of mine. Would it vanish as I grew colder, waiting there? Would my lungs frost over; would I fade into some new form? My matter didn't seem to, here up against this brick wall beneath a starless sky.

The stagnant water had begun to ice over, but the process was slow. That thin layer could not stop the trickle of fluid stink from creeping slickly below.

*   *   *

The first night she spent, I woke with peonies crushed within my fists and a thistle on my tongue.

Who says flowers are supple and soft? The flowers I have known are acts of violence. Put your faith in something that can look back at you when you stare into its face.

"Your dream is keeping you," she told me in the dark of early dawn. "The only way to leave is to let it go yourself."

And I am back with her; that is a dream in itself. Her voice is a twist of green tendrils, bright like poison, alluring like spindles or a locked box. This house, with its clocks out of sync and no screens on the windows, might as well be a flowering vine. Not a step I take here can be solid; tentative, I check for thorns along the way, careful to avoid treading on pain and poison alike.

"How long was I out?" I want to know.

Her smile, red like a broad, dark daisy under moonlight. There is something hidden there, something I will never touch with hand or eye.

"Some dreams never release." Her voice has nectar in it; bees take in more than they give when they make honey, I recall from a book I glanced through once and have since forgotten.

The walls might be wax cells. I can see through them, see out into the dawn as it expands and the harshness of sunlight cuts across everything, waking or not.

I am trying to let go.

*   *   *

Art has never been my diversion of choice. There is something sinister in a static moment, painted or sculpted, even photographed. Without context, without what comes before and after, what can a person say that will be believed?

"It's time for me to move on," she'd said, staring up at a canvas. Its base was level with her mouth, and she had to tilt her head towards the sky to see it.

I have always been a rooted thing myself. I cannot fly or swim, but I never lose a sense of the ground beneath me.

"From what?"

From me, I thought. *From us.*

The words glowed in the air between us, buzzing and flickering orange as she spoke them. "To what. To something new."

"Without me."

"You could wait, if you want to. I won't ask, though; it's up to you."

The stink of stagnance in our shared breath during that first kiss was inscribed within me from that moment, and I knew where I would end up. We had never shared anything but the air that night, I knew.

Not really, I remind myself as a fourth hour rounds and that pause the world takes before dawn keeps me suspended with everything else. There had been nothing solid between us. Like flowers, we folded then crumbled into nothing but the memory of something colorful and vibrant.

All that dead matter beneath lends itself to lush growth: when we're dirt, food, shit, and bodies (that intake, export those same things), all become as one. Peel back the layers of a canvas and you'll find yourself with a hollow frame, fabric strips, crumbling clumps of paint and crooked staples at your feet.

Look, what a mess you've made.

Husband

Delila couldn't sleep through the night no matter how hard she tried. She'd have to stop drinking water at noon if she was going to make it through without waking up to pee at least once. She'd been to two doctors, neither of whom had been of any help; the second one had patronizingly asked if she made a habit of "creating reasons" to book medical appointments.

She wasn't a fucking hypochondriac. She just wanted some sleep.

That night, she rolled off the bed without bothering to glance towards her husband, Henry, in the dark. Some nights, she would look over at him and hope the sound of his even, restful breathing might lull her back to sleep, although her bladder always seemed to win out.

Henry didn't snore; it was something small and silly she'd bragged to all her friends about years back when they'd first gotten engaged. She had boasted that she would always be able to sleep through the night, her peacefully snoozing husband laying quietly at her side.

Maybe that's what this bladder thing was: karma for being such a braggart.

Delila sat on the cold toilet seat, wondering why everything felt worse in the late hours of the night. The edges of the tile floor beneath her feet seemed less smooth than they did in daylight, and her hair stuck to her neck in odd clumps that felt like spiders on her skin.

She flushed and stumbled back towards bed, and as she settled under the covers, the body next to hers turned over, perhaps in response to all her moving about. Then, a low snore began in the darkness.

"Henry?" she murmured in confusion, and when the snoring grew louder, she repeated her husband's name in a more agitated tone. "Henry, wake up—you're snoring."

Was this some kind of sick joke? Her husband, who ordinarily slept like a kitten, sounded like a hibernating bear.

"Henry!"

The formerly sleeping man now turned back towards her, and in a voice Delila had never before heard in her life, asked, "Who the hell's Henry?"

*   *   *

"Delila, do you know where you are?"

She blinked incredulously at the paramedic looking into her face, his tone calm and his words slow as though he were speaking to a child having a tantrum. His eyes were calculating, though, scrutinizing and evaluating her as the moments passed.

"I'm in my fucking house," she snapped, "on my fucking sofa, waiting for someone to tell me where the fuck my husband is. Do you know where *you* are?"

The paramedic looked over to the man Delila had encountered in the middle of the night, the man who'd been lying where Henry should have been. He shrugged helplessly.

"What is your husband's name, Delila?" the paramedic continued.

"Henry," she said. "It's Henry Beauchamp."

"Sweetheart," the man told her, "my name is Scott. Scott Ryan, and you're Delila Ryan. It's Scott, it's...it's me!"

She said nothing, just stared in fear at this stranger who was insisting that he knew her. Finding him in bed with her had been terrifying enough; after she'd sprinted away from him, he'd only managed to convince her to unlock the bathroom door by calling the paramedics as soon as dawn had hit, when the sound of other voices offered her some small hope.

But for those hours she'd been locked in the bathroom, Delila had sat shaking in the tub, wondering: where was Henry? Where was her husband? How had he disappeared in mere moments, when she stumbled to the bathroom as she did in the middle of every night? And who would see her through this if he was nowhere to be found?

"We've been married for eight years, honey." Scott shoved a hand through his hair in apparent frustration. "I just—I don't understand what you're trying to achieve here, Didi."

She stood bolt upright at the sound of Henry's nickname for her. "Who are you? Where's Henry? *Where is my husband?*"

"All right, all right." The paramedic gently but firmly brought her back down to the sofa. Tantrum or not, he seemed determined to remain professional. "Let's try some other questions, Delila. Do you know what day it is?"

She fought the urge to smack him, tried to remember that he was only asking her questions because this strange man had called and told him that she was crazy, and acting crazy wasn't going to help matters. "It's Tuesday, November first."

"Good. And where are we right now?"

"I told you," she said, struggling to keep her patience, "we're in my house."

"Can I have an address?"

"111 Maple Drive. It's been our house for the past decade, mine and Henry's."

The paramedic nodded and looked again at the strange man.

"Didi, our house is number 110," he said, his voice softening as he seemed to regard her with increasing concern. "There is no 111 on Maple—we're the last house on the side with the even numbers."

"No," Delila said through gritted teeth, "no, we're last on the side with the odd numbers. It's why my husband always plays 111 on his lottery card."

"I play 110," Scott offered helplessly to the paramedic.

"Okay," the paramedic said, standing up, "I'm suggesting we get you to the hospital so the doctors there can talk with you, Delila."

Tears started streaming from her eyes. "I don't need a doctor," she said. "I need my husband!"

"I'm right here, baby. Why can't you see that I'm right here?"

"Mr. Ryan, your wife needs medical attention. She's missing basic things that you say she knew yesterday. We don't know what we're dealing with here, and we won't until we get to the hospital and talk to a doctor." He turned back to Delila. "I'm not going to lie to you: I'm concerned about you right now."

"That makes two of us," she told him, her voice shakier than she wanted it to be.

"Are you going to agree to go to the hospital?"

She watched in bewildered fear as Scott, the stranger, walked over to the bowl where Henry kept his car keys and picked them up. "Only if I can ride with you."

Scott turned to look at her with hurt in his eyes, but the paramedic seemed to expect this. "That's not a problem, Delila. I'll be with you the whole time."

She nodded slowly, never taking her eyes off this man claiming to be her husband. Delila didn't trust him for a second, but a hospital couldn't hurt. After all, hospitals were official buildings that held records and offered an air of authority. A little authority might be just the thing to help her figure out what the hell was going on.

But the hospital was not the saving grace Delila had hoped it would be. No matter how she pleaded with the nurses and doctors to look into her husband, to find a way to contact him, this man Scott Ryan's word seemed to matter more than hers. She heard different terms floating about while she was there, none of which helped her: amnesia, dementia, trauma, shock.

Once she realized she was getting nowhere, Delila took to observing this man who claimed to be married to her. He didn't seem like a psychopath or a con artist; the whole time, he kept sending worried glances in her direction, appearing genuinely concerned about her wellbeing. He even demonstrated a nervous habit of sorts: he had a silver coin that he kept flipping between his fingers as he spoke with hospital staff, asked and answered questions, responded with things he should have no way of knowing about her.

As the doctors spoke less and less to her and increasingly about her, Delila thought on how different Scott was from Henry. That was what was especially strange about this situation: not only did she not know the man who insisted he was her husband, but he also seemed to be the opposite of the man she'd actually married. Henry was slight and kind, calm and thoughtful. Scott was large and loud, and he kept fidgeting, his movements expressing agitation more than anything else. The coin must have turned over in his hands a few hundred times from when they'd arrived at the hospital.

In the end, Delila was sent home with a stranger, and there was nothing she could do about it.

*   *   *

Everything was wrong. It was all there, it just wasn't how it should have been, how it was supposed to be.

"How are you doing today?" Scott greeted her in his gruff voice, which had been his habit since they'd returned from the hospital.

Delila fought the tears that had been rising in her for the past week. This was ridiculous, she reminded herself: Scott was some impostor, some sort of conman who had taken Henry from her and was fooling everyone around them. She couldn't be crazy; the doctors had found nothing in her scans, no head injury, nothing to suggest she'd gotten a strange illness that could cause confusion. She was too young for dementia, and although the idea of traumatic shock had been raised, the only trauma she'd undergone was losing the husband no one seemed to believe existed. Delila knew she wasn't losing her mind—there was nothing to say that she was but for this inexplicable man!

Except there were things that weren't making sense to her. She'd seen the numbers on the front of her house, right where they'd always been, except the last digit was indeed a zero, as Scott had insisted. The curtains in the living room had a rose trim, when she'd deliberately chosen lavender in memory of her favorite aunt who had loved the color. The tree in their backyard was an oak when it should have been a maple, and the pansies Delila had planted in front of the house had somehow been replaced with begonias. They were all small things,

things that someone might not notice if they weren't scrutinizing an entire life that seemed just slightly off.

And then there was Scott himself. He wasn't a small thing at all. Facing her with hopeful concern, she still couldn't reply to him as she searched his eyes for something, some tell that would explain the past hellish days to her. He knew things about her that he shouldn't, that she'd only ever told her husband. Delila was sickened that she'd found herself grateful as the week had passed: that he never fought with her, though he did contradict half the things she said; that he'd taken the sofa without complaint, allowing her to sleep alone in her bed, the bed she had shared with Henry for the past twelve years of their lives.

What riled her the most, though—what she hated beyond anything—was the sneaky, nasty question that kept rising in the back of her mind: was it possible that she was wrong?

It felt like a betrayal of the worst kind to Henry, the husband she knew, the husband she loved. And yet there it was, in every quiet moment when she tried to make sense of things: the house number, the curtains, the tree, the flowers.

Had she lost something? Had her mind created a life she thought she knew and covered up a life she'd actually led? Had it fabricated the love of that life?

"Didi? You...okay?"

She cleared her throat. Whatever was going on, she hadn't lost sense of the woman she believed herself to be, and that woman was resilient even under duress. "Yes, thanks."

*   *   *

After two weeks had passed, Delila was beginning to come to terms with the fact that Henry Beauchamp, the man she thought she'd loved for the past decade, might be a figment of a mind she could no longer trust, despite the fact that it was her own.

She and Scott were sitting in the living room. Delila had noticed more changes, more things that hadn't seemed right to her, like the handles on the small chest of drawers they kept full of throw blankets in case the room got cold in the evenings. She'd always believed them to be brass knobs, but they were silver and flat, not unlike the coin Scott always seemed to trouble.

He was doing that right now as he awkwardly tried to fill the silence between them. "So..."

Delila sighed. She didn't blame him for being at a loss for words. He'd tried to say anything and everything that might help over the past two weeks.

"I don't understand what's going on," she said, not for the first time.

Scott nodded, the coin playing between the fingers of his left hand.

"But," she added, and she saw his eyebrows lift in surprise, "I'm not completely out of touch with reality. It's clear that...that my mind is not aligning with everything that's been happening over the past two weeks. I don't know why that is, but I want to try and move forward."

Traitor, her heart screamed as dozens of images of Henry, beautiful and easygoing Henry, flashed through her mind. How could she give him up? And to what? To the idea that she was insane, that her life and everything in it had been a fabrication?

"Didi, I love you as much as I always have," Scott said, his husky voice heavy with apparent emotion. "I need you to know that. I don't blame you for any of this. It's been hard, but I know none of this is something you've chosen. And I support you, one hundred percent, just like I always have."

She nodded now, not trusting her voice.

"I'm going to do whatever you need, be whatever you need," he went on. "And if what you need is to get to know me all over again, then that's what we'll do. We'll date. I'll take you out—I got you to fall in love with me once, didn't I? I'm sure it can happen again."

He looked so hopeful, so uncharacteristically soft in that moment that Delila found she couldn't bring herself to look away from him.

"Okay," she whispered. "Okay...Scott. I'll try. I promise I'm going to try."

*   *   *

And date they did. Scott took her all sorts of places that Henry never would have: amusement parks and rock-climbing gyms, hockey games and bowling alleys. Henry—or the false memories that everyone seemed to agree were Henry—had enjoyed picnics on the beach, walks through parks and botanical gardens, museum and gallery openings.

Scott always seemed to need an adrenaline rush to enjoy himself, something fast and loud that made her heart race faster than she was used to. At one point, sitting beside him on a rollercoaster that was much more intricate than she would have liked, Delila thought maybe she did have trauma from all of the breakneck shit her apparent husband had roped her into over the course of a decade. Maybe that's why her mind had invented Henry; it needed to slow down so she might catch her breath.

But she'd never needed to catch her breath more than she had over the past month. She still couldn't accept that this was her life, even if she'd decided to believe it. All of her friends seemed to know and love Scott, as did her own family, and Delila knew that such an overwhelming majority made hers the odd delusion out. Still, her heart could not reconcile with what she'd made her mind resign itself to.

And so when Scott began to kiss her, a piece of her would recoil. Delila fought hard not to let this show, not wanting to hurt her husband's feelings—how would she feel if Henry had been in her place, and she'd been the one who had been imagined? And it wasn't all that hard; if anything, she experienced a second adolescence, where the person she was with fumbled gracelessly around her body and she pretended not to mind.

The first night they slept together, though, she had to choke back bile and a feeling of utter defeat. If she'd been thinking during their days together that Scott was the opposite of Henry, this act cemented that reality.

Exhausted, aching, and unsatisfied, she fell almost instantly asleep in the aftermath, thinking of how the look on Scott's face throughout had been startling, if not frightening. His eyes had been full of a kind of cold victory, and the light from the street lamps outside had made them flash like silver in the dark.

*   *   *

Delila woke up to pee that night. Still sore and now desperately uncomfortable, she made her way to the bathroom.

She sat heavily on the seat, sighing through sleep and sadness. The world might have forced her to accept Henry had never existed, but that didn't mean she loved him any less. And as far as her memory knew, the last time she'd been with him had been in the late hours of a night just like this, lying together in bed until her bladder betrayed her and life as she knew it had been ripped away.

Did she dare hope that when she returned to bed, she'd find things back to normal?

As she left the bathroom, a silver circle gleamed then darkened, gleamed, darkened, as Scott played with the coin from the bed.

Delila hovered in the bathroom doorway, feeling the room behind her where she'd hidden from this man on the first day she'd met him. Something in the air felt charged; there was a clarity she was experiencing, and in a moment, it seemed to undo all of the persuasion she'd thrown upon herself over the past weeks. It said that she knew what was real, and she'd known all along, and with it came a wave of rage at all she'd had to endure.

What was it with that coin? That stupid fucking coin he kept flipping. Henry would never have toyed with a coin like that, her thoughts snapped. They came from the part of her mind that had been furious with her since the first day Scott had appeared, that had all along been inciting her to loathe herself for accepting an impostor in place of her husband, her *real* husband.

The only thing worse than losing Henry might be betraying him.

"I'm so glad that we're finally putting all of this shit behind us," Scott said, still flipping the coin as he gave her that odd, wolfish smile of his. "I mean, I know it's been hell on you, Didi, but it hasn't been so easy for me, either."

"I know."

"I'm just glad that I have you now, that you're convinced again that this life is ours."

She frowned, and something in her began to grow louder, to make her blood run cold at the sight of this man who mere weeks ago had been a stranger in her bed. It was rushing through her ears, reminding her that the detail with which she'd remembered her life with Henry—every miniscule moment, each fleeting gesture, everything she could recall—none of that could be faked, could it? The noise that roared inside her said a sick mind couldn't, especially in such detail, achieve the depth to which she had lived her life with a man that was not this one in front of her.

The screaming inside her was doubt, and Delila knew it was also the truth.

Scott didn't move as she began to stumble backwards, as she fumbled to grab a lamp from the bedroom dresser. He even chuckled a little as she raised it, as she realized this was not real; the threat of the man before her was, his presence in the room that was *almost* her bedroom, *almost* her house, all of that was real, but this life? This life was a mockery of her real life, a life that did not include this man. It was a shoddy facsimile, an imitation that had taken her in its thrall, but at the end of the day, Delila could recognize her own life and *this was not it.*

"Who the fuck are you?" she hissed.

And he flipped the coin one last time, its silver gleam reflecting in his eyes as he smiled, predatory beyond question, and told her in a voice that sounded like shattering glass, "Now, let's lay this all to rest."

OUTAGES

Bits

Charlotte entered the lobby of her apartment building. As she caught a glimpse of herself in the mirror-paneled walls, she found the night black and empty behind her. But despite the hush of winter and the absence of anyone else nearby, a strange scraping sound seemed to follow her inside. She turned to look behind her, checked the mirrors again and saw no soul reflected but her own. The scraping continued. It was an eerily gentle sound, just present enough to be disturbing. A smile of relief broke the tension in her face as she realized it was coming from the bottom of her own right shoe.

There Charlotte found a tiny bit of what must be toilet paper, though she hadn't entered a bathroom since leaving home. She scraped her toe against the lobby rug, and the small gray bit was left behind. Suddenly, she seemed to feel the cold from outside, which had until now not permeated her warm wrap of a winter coat. Pulling it closer, she hurriedly made her way to the elevator.

"Hey!" A sharp pain glanced the gloved finger that had pressed the elevator button. Another bit of—was it tissue? It couldn't be toilet paper stuck to her fingertip now. She hadn't been anywhere near toilet paper for hours, certainly hadn't handled any with her gloves on. She shook her hand, and the scrap of tissue reluctantly fell away.

Charlotte shivered as she stepped into the elevator that would take her to her apartment. "Hopefully, the heat will be on in there," she complained. The echo of her own words told her the lobby was still empty. She carefully used her knuckle to hit the button for the tenth floor, wary of her still throbbing fingertip. But there was no pain this time.

The elevator lights flickered, and Charlotte shifted her weight anxiously. A hollowness lingered in the leg she'd been favoring, and she looked down to find a few more bits of—it *had* to be tissue, didn't it? What else could it be? Now she scrubbed with her hand at her leg, slapping away scraps which again seemed to want to stick before resolving to float down to the elevator floor.

"Where are these coming from?" She turned out the pockets of her coat but found no tissues there, not even a candy wrapper or grocery receipt.

The elevator seemed to yawn upwards, and Charlotte considered hitting another button and trying her luck with the stairs. "At this rate, that would be faster," she said, and the words were faint as though they, too, felt the cold. And because she'd grown chilly enough to start trembling, she pressed the button for eight.

Another shiver came, across her side this time. In the tiny mirrored faces of the elevator buttons, Charlotte saw something underneath her arm, light and papery against her charcoal grey coat. Shaking no longer from cold, she glanced down to find several more bits resting there.

This time, she didn't wipe them off.

"I just need to get home." Her voice shook as the elevator finally opened onto the eighth floor and she stepped out, making a sharp left towards the stairwell. The door to the stairs stuck. Charlotte's left toes were tingling now, and she slammed her hands against the door and finally made it through.

The sole bulb on the stairwell wall was flickering.

"Really?" The word was quick, but as it emerged, Charlotte realized in horror that the center of her tongue had gone cold, and she gagged on something that crinkled within her mouth. She struggled and spat, and as the gray bits finally fell like malformed snowflakes from her lips, she tasted the telltale metallic tang of blood beneath another cutting flash of pain.

She lifted her right foot to start up the stairs, shaking violently. But the bits or flakes of—what the hell was this?! They started to accumulate as she pushed her way up: there were two at her right ankle, kissed with an icy tremor; then three on her left toe, still tingling as though numb. A small cluster atop her right foot; a line extending up her left calf; and when she stepped again onto her right foot, it buckled. Charlotte cried out, choking on more of those impossible and painful bits that came from her throat, her feet, the hands that painfully grasped the stairs, the skin that scraped as she slid down.

She crawled upwards, desperate to be home, sure that if she could just reach the tenth floor—if she could just get into her cozy apartment where nothing had ever hurt her or made her bleed on a cold night—surely there she would find safety from this indescribable assault. More bits built upon those she'd shed, and with each that was scraped from her buckling, dragging form, Charlotte felt searing pain.

"Please," she begged, the word muffled from so much crinkling in her mouth. "Please, please."

The bulb flickered brightly as she managed her way to the top step, and then, with an electric hum, it popped and went dark.

*   *   *

The next day, Charlotte's neighbor Michelle left her tenth-floor apartment and decided to take the stairs, as she often did so she might get an early start on her steps for the day. She opened the stairwell door and began her descent, her morning coffee still singing in her blood.

But when she reached the middle of the stairs between the tenth and ninth floors, she suddenly stopped. On the platform leading to the ninth floor, there was an enormous pile of—what was it? Paper waste? Shredded tissue?

"Ugh." Refusing to dirty her work clothes before the day had even begun by walking through such a bizarre mess, Michelle turned on her heel to head back up to the elevator. She did not notice the tiny bit that was now stuck to the bottom of her right shoe.

The Hum

It wasn't Maria's first time working in a library, but even a week after she started, she could tell that the job was going to be different.

She'd been a page during college. Whenever you tell someone you're a page in a library, reactions range from puzzlement to mild amusement, as though you're *so* excited about working with books, you've lost your identity and have confused yourself with the objects themselves. But a library page is mainly a shelver: you put the books back where they're supposed to be and help the librarians with small tasks here and there. Nothing so glamorous as an identity crisis and nothing that will get a person much in terms of savings or healthcare, but a job nonetheless.

Maria applied to the Glass Library two weeks after she'd moved to Ashland. She hadn't planned on the move, but got caught in a whirlwind of bad luck: school ended and she got a secretarial job and moved in with her boyfriend; then her relationship ended and she moved in with a friend from college; then her friend got engaged the same week Maria lost her secretarial job and she was fucked. She had no family left and she had to go somewhere, so she thought of all the places her friends from college had mentioned had cheap rents. Ashland was the closest.

When she checked the town's library website, thinking she could get another paging job before finding something with better pay and maybe even benefits, Maria was surprised to see that the Glass Library had an open call for new employees. The only thing an interested person needed to do was submit to a background check. As for previous library experience, the job description called it a "bonus, but not necessary for employment at the Glass Library." She sent in her résumé, hoping that this so-called bonus in her work history might give her an edge.

A day later, she had an interview.

"What brings you to Ashland, Maria?" the man who'd introduced himself as Library Director Mitch Hudgins asked after they'd settled down in a quiet room.

"Oh, I had to move," she answered, wanting to kick herself for being unprepared for such a basic question. Interviews were always like that, though: you wanted money to live, but had to pretend the job interested you for shinier reasons.

But Mitch Hudgins nodded as though that made a lot of sense, then gestured to her résumé with a smile. "I see you spent four years working at another library?"

"As a page," she offered unhelpfully. To say her interview skills were rusty would have been overgenerous.

"Yes, I see," Mitch Hudgins murmured. "Well, I'm afraid we're much too small to have roles like clerks and pages. The Glass Library has staffers, and those staffers split the work among them. We don't hire part time; everyone's salaried because everyone pitches in. Would you be willing to take on more responsibility than just shelving books, Maria?"

"Of course, Director Hudgins."

Now he laughed. "Oh! That's something. But no, no, please: you'll call me Mitch. Everyone does—even the patrons!"

"Sorry...Mitch. Of course, I'd be happy to take on more responsibility."

"Well, that's fine. That's just fine." He studied her for a moment. "What do you think of Ashland, Maria?"

She shrugged, feeling more relaxed now that she knew this job might last longer than an emergency hustle. "It seems nice. I've only been here a couple of weeks, but everyone I've met has been pleasant."

He raised an eyebrow. "And you've met a lot of people?"

She blushed. "Um, everyone I've met at the grocery store has been really pleasant?"

"That sounds more like it," Mitch chuckled. "Well, I'd be the last one to put you off our small gem of a town. Ashland's a special place in that the folks who do get adjusted to life here are, as you put it, quite pleasant."

There was a long moment where Mitch's gaze drifted back down to the résumé and he was silent. Maria cleared her throat. "Did you have any questions? About my résumé, I mean?"

"Hmm? Oh, no, no. You're a shoo-in, if I'm going to be honest. We need the help, and it's clear you've got a good head on your shoulders. It's just..." Again he paused, choosing his words carefully. "It's good you're already feeling at home in town. Some of our patrons have a little more trouble making that adjustment. Even folks born and raised here can end up having difficulty now and then. And I just want you to understand that, here at the library, we support everyone—including people having the hardest time."

"Of course," Maria said, nodding as though she understood. She assumed Mitch might be talking his way around homelessness, since libraries were so crucial to those communities. At her previous job, the director had been kind and progressive, and no one was allowed to chase anybody away who came into the library. They'd even had a social worker on staff.

Before she could offer any of this as reassurance, though, Mitch stood. "Why don't I introduce you to the rest of the staff?"

"Really?" He'd said she was a shoo-in, but she was surprised. Her last job had required an Excel test before she even finished the interview. "Now?"

"Sure, why not? You'll have to meet them sooner or later, and everybody's here. Come on, I'll show you around."

Maria followed her new boss through the library. Mitch waxed poetic about how everyone pulled their weight, though staff tended to specialize in different departments based on their talents. She didn't say much, taking in her environment as they walked. The number of floor-to-ceiling windows was impressive; for a small-town library, Maria thought, they must have a huge budget to afford such a nice building, even if it wasn't all that big.

There was something about the windows that particularly impressed her, though she couldn't quite understand what it was. They were somehow more imposing, more notable than they should have been. That didn't make sense, but she didn't have a chance to dwell on it, because Mitch cleared his throat and suddenly called out loudly, "Hey, do you all think you can come over here for a second?"

Maria jumped, not expecting the man to start shouting. But the handful of people seated at tables paid Mitch no mind as they paged through their books and newspapers. And, she realized, his voice hadn't really resonated. She didn't see any soundproofing in the room, but had she not been standing right next to Mitch, she might not have realized he'd yelled at all.

"Now, we've been looking for staff, as you all know," Mitch began, once the five people who'd been working in the library had gathered. "Maria here is going to join us starting next week."

She nodded in confirmation, even though she technically hadn't accepted the job yet.

"Maria, this is Ellen, whose specialty is working behind the circulation desk because she's the only one here who can ask someone for money and not make them even a little mad."

Everyone chuckled at that. Ellen, a mild-looking woman in her late fifties, gave Maria a small smile.

"José and Gillian usually work the stacks," Mitch went on, gesturing to a lanky kid who couldn't have hit drinking age yet and a woman who might have been in her early thirties, though she was dressed in a matronly skirt suit more formal than what any of her coworkers wore, including Mitch. José offered a smile, as Ellen had, but Gillian frowned a little.

"What does Maria specialize in?" she wanted to know.

"Well, she actually did a bit of shelving at another library once upon a time," Mitch said. "So she'll probably spend a good amount of time in the stacks with you two."

Whatever hesitation Gillian had felt upon Maria's introduction dissipated, and she crossed her arms in approval. "Good, because Annette keeps messing the magazines up. We could use some help."

"I told you, if someone would just write it down for me, I could get it." Another woman—short, slim-shouldered, and likely in her sixties—looked down at the floor, clearly embarrassed by Gillian's words.

"That's all right, now," Mitch quickly broke in. "Annette's great with the kids that come in, Maria. She does at least half our storytimes, and lord knows I'm more concerned with those than with the magazine section."

Annette gave a glance so bashful it was almost sheepish, and Maria decided it couldn't hurt to befriend someone who'd just gotten verbally shit on in front of her. "I'll be learning where everything goes, too. Maybe we can tackle magazines together."

Gillian rolled her eyes, but José said, "Now we have no choice but to map out the floor, Gill. It'll help the newbie, and besides, even we get rusty on where things go now and then."

"Speak for yourself," Gillian told him, but she didn't say anything else to Annette.

"Aren't you going to introduce me, Mitch?"

The last woman present, who had been watching every interaction with thoughtful eyes, turned her gaze Maria's way.

"How could I leave you out, Shirl?" Mitch grinned. "Maria, this is Shirley. If we really have someone running the place, I know it isn't me!"

"Come now, Mitch—we'd be lost without you. You direct things."

Mitch laughed again, though Maria wasn't sure that he should. She'd thought there was a sly note of unkindness in Shirley's last remark, a hint of mockery that indicated Mitch didn't do very much at all. But the woman's expression didn't change, so Maria figured maybe she was hearing things.

"What do you do, Shirley?" she asked, trying to be polite. The woman set her on edge, with her focused gaze and unreadable face.

"I tend to be the one who opens and closes, though we all have keys. And I write much of the material the library puts out to the public—flyers, newsletters, calendars, all of that. In fact, I'd be thrilled to have some help in that department, if you've got any typing skills." Her smile never wavered as she spoke.

"I worked as a secretary before I moved here."

"Wonderful."

There was a moment of awkward silence, and Maria noticed Annette shifting uncomfortably. Shirley's gaze flickered to the older woman a few times, but otherwise, Maria remained under her passive scrutiny.

"Okay, well, I've got paperwork for our new hire," Mitch said, breaking the palpable pause. "And I'm sure the rest of you have work to do."

Everyone began returning to the stacks and desks around the library, but Annette hesitated and then jogged over.

"Um, Mitch?"

"Hmm?" Mitch turned around and seemed to register whatever was on the older woman's face. "Oh, Annette...is this about...?"

"I'm sorry to bother you, but I just don't know what else to do."

"We're having Tony and his guys check the caulking on all the windows this weekend, I promise."

"And the doors?" Annette asked anxiously. She ran a hand through the hair on the side of her head, and catching a flash of orange, Maria realized she was wearing earplugs.

"The doors too, Annette." Mitch gave an encouraging smile, but Maria could see there was a strange note of sympathy in his eyes.

Annette nodded, then made her way back towards the children's space, narrow shoulders slumped with what seemed to be intense worry.

"Is there something wrong with the windows?" Maria asked, curious.

Mitch seemed about to give an answer that he was again having trouble finding the right words for. Then he shook his head. "No. Not with the windows, no."

She followed him up to his office and received no further explanation.

*   *   *

"What did you major in during college, Maria?"

Shirley had come up behind her so silently that Maria jumped and almost hit her head on the shelf above where she'd been working, reading call numbers in search of misshelved books.

"Um, I was a dual major. English and Sociology."

"Really?"

"Yeah. Why?"

She tutted. "I was just surprised by the descriptions you wrote for next month's newsletter."

It was Maria's third day on the job. So far, she'd shadowed her coworkers to start learning the computer systems, the layout of the library, and the daily tasks the staff performed. There was some light cleaning to do each day, consisting mostly of emptying garbage bins and wiping down tables and chairs. Mitch employed a professional cleaning service that came in each weekend to do the real work. Maria worked alongside José, Gillian, Ellen, and Annette, observing them and taking suggestions as she went.

When she'd shadowed Shirley, though, she'd been instructed to type up a portion of the newsletter that was meant to go out the following month. Shirley didn't even remain in the room while Maria worked on it. Although she'd been apprehensive about taking on such a big responsibility on only her second day, her new coworker had insisted. And now, she'd apparently read over Maria's work.

"Surprised by the descriptions how?" Maria asked. She still wasn't comfortable with Shirley. No one else seemed to mind her—not that they had much cause to interact with the woman, since she spent the bulk of her days behind a desk in back. But there was something about her watchful eyes that made Maria's skin crawl like someone had dropped a spider down the back of her shirt.

"They weren't nearly as polished as I'd expected: unnecessarily wordy and a little sloppy, actually." She gave that cold, unwavering smile Maria was growing familiar with.

"I...I'm sorry," Maria replied, doing her best to employ all of the skills she'd used with unpleasant coworkers in her last job. "I can give it another try, if you'd like."

"Oh, good. You should do that." Shirley turned and went back to her computer.

"Weird," Maria muttered as José came by, pushing a cart of nonfiction.

"Everything okay today?" he asked.

She nodded, figuring it was better not to try and explain the interaction she'd just had with Shirley, since she didn't entirely understand it herself. "Just shelf-reading while things are quiet."

"Well, don't get too cozy—word is it's going to rain." He grinned. "We get the highest traffic when it rains in the middle of the day."

"That makes sense. Hey, José..."

"Yeah?"

Maria hesitated. "I don't want to gossip or anything. And I mean, it's not even a big deal. I just have a question about..."

He lowered his voice. "Annette?"

She was surprised. Aside from a pleasant hour together of sanitizing toys with antibacterial wipes and putting wooden puzzles away in the children's section, Maria had barely had a chance to work with Annette at all. "Uh..."

José nodded. "I'm not surprised you noticed. But you should know, she's a great person otherwise."

"Okay." She tried to act as though she knew what he was talking about.

"It's this town, if you ask me," he went on. "One person catches another talking about hearing it, and then it's just infectious."

"Hearing it?"

He shrugged. "I know, it's strange—you figure enough people hear something, it's got to mean there's something to hear, right? But I mean, I've never picked up a thing myself, and I'm a 'seeing is believing' kind of guy. Or hearing. Whatever."

Maria nodded, but she was getting more confused the longer this conversation went on.

"Anyway, try to be patient with Annette," José said. "She's harmless, and just got caught up in the whole Ashland drama of it all. I'd say every ten or so patrons you meet, you'll find one who hears it, too."

"Really."

José nodded, then his eyes caught on something behind her. "Wow, it started earlier than they said it would."

Maria turned and saw that the rain José had mentioned was falling outside the library. Lightning flashed and water poured like buckets, splashing up from the pavement in bursts of gathering puddles. She was glad they were in the library, safe and dry from the deluge, tucked into the silence of the stacks.

And that was when she realized: she hadn't known it was raining until José had told her. She hadn't heard a thunder clap or drops against the windowpanes; in fact, beyond the silence of the library in which they stood, she hadn't heard a thing.

"José," she said, fighting a chill along her spine that reminded her of interacting with Shirley, "why isn't there any sound from outside?"

"Like I said, a lot of people think they hear it," he murmured. "The library has done everything it can to be a kind of sanctuary for folks dealing with it. Mitch reinforces the soundproofing all the time. He has specialists come in on weekends, and they're always putting in more caulking."

Maria remembered how Annette had approached Mitch, how he'd promised the weekend crew would check on the windows and doors. She recalled the first glimpse she'd caught of Annette's orange earplugs, which the woman seemed to wear every day. And although she didn't understand the extent of it, Maria knew one thing for sure: her coworker Annette was hearing something, and she wasn't the only one.

She waited for José to walk into the stacks, for the rhythmic repetitive squeak of the cart's wheels to vanish along with him. She stood as still as she could, closed her eyes, tried to quiet her breathing. She didn't move for ten, twenty, twenty-five seconds. And even with the rain she'd seen thundering down outside, she could not hear a thing.

When Maria opened her eyes to check that the storm was still in progress, she realized something else: that quality in the Glass Library that she couldn't quite put her finger on, the thing that had struck her as somehow distinct about the windows, was the thickness of the glass. The windows all around the library had to be at least four or five inches thick. It wasn't something easy to spot day to day, but now, with raindrops trickling down outside and the odd flyer that had been taped to the interior glass for patrons to read, it was obvious. She didn't think she'd ever seen glass so thick.

That night, Maria poked around on the internet, trying to figure out what it was that Annette and the other patrons José had told her about could hear that she apparently couldn't. Eventually, she found forums discussing what people called "the hum," a sound that was driving many in the discussion threads to seek medical and psychiatric help. She read tale after tale of sleep destroyed, marriages ruined, even loss of custody for some parents. Whatever the Ashland hum might be, it was actively wrecking the lives of more than a few people who lived there.

She was too tired to keep reading, but figured she might have a chance to do a little digging at work. After all, what was the point of working in a small-town library if you didn't access local archives every once in a while?

*   *   *

By the end of her first week, Maria managed to learn more about Ashland and the hum, though not as much as she would have liked because it turned out that the unofficial archivist at the Glass Library was Shirley. Maria was avoiding her as much as possible, so she had to rely on conversations with other coworkers and patrons to discover more.

She began to take note of when people who came into the library behaved oddly. One man pulled at his ear continually as he sat over a newspaper Maria wasn't even sure he was reading. Another person came in with a huge pair of what looked like pricey headphones, until she realized that they weren't plugged into anything. There was the chance that they might have been wireless, but she didn't think so.

That Friday, Annette was leading a morning storytime and offered to let her sit in. Maria was delighted to get a break from shelf-reading and entering new items into the catalog, which had already become monotonous work. After half an hour of stories, singing, dancing, and coloring, she felt a sense of calm she hadn't had since the day of the rainstorm, and she thanked Annette for welcoming her into the class.

"Oh, it's no trouble," Annette said with a watery smile as they packed up crayons and stray coloring sheets. "You were great with the kids. I could tell they liked you."

"How long have you worked here?" Maria asked. She was curious about her new coworker who apparently could hear something that no matter how she tried, she could not.

"Well, let's see. I left the daycare about two months after my sister died, so that would make it...three years?"

"I'm sorry," Maria said. "About your sister, I mean."

"I miss her, but she was having a lot of trouble. I don't know how much time she would have had, even if winter hadn't gotten to her."

"She was sick?"

Annette's face closed a little. "No, she was sensitive. Like me."

Some of the coloring sheets she'd been carrying slipped from her hands, and Maria bent to retrieve them.

"You're a nice person," Annette commented. "My sister was a nice person, too."

"Thanks."

"Hmm. I don't know if I mean that in the way you think."

They were closing up the storytime room and heading back into the children's stacks, and Maria lowered her voice so she wouldn't disturb anyone. "Well, what did you mean?"

Annette sighed. "You haven't heard anything since you moved to Ashland, have you? Anything that's maybe keeping you up at night? Making it hard for you to focus?"

Maria shook her head. It was so strange to her, the idea that many people in the same town could hear the same thing, but that as far as anyone knew, there was nothing to hear to begin with.

Annette nodded. "That's all right. You're better off that way."

"Um," Maria began, not wanting to overstep, "can I ask you what it's like?"

Annette's sad eyes took on a haunted aspect. "It's awful. It's like the sound of all your hopes just slipping away. At least, that's how it is for me. Winifred—my sister—she said it was like something in the corner of her eye at all moments that never left her alone but that she could never see clearly. She couldn't focus on anything, in the end. Most of us can't."

"Is that why you left the daycare you mentioned?"

She nodded again. "It was making me so erratic at work, and I was worried about my ability to watch the kids. And then Winifred was gone, and the sadness was just too much."

"How did you end up at the library?"

"A lot of people who hear it come in here for some peace. It's not perfect, but Mitch has done what he can to block it out as much as possible. I was already here a lot, and when I told Mitch I'd lost my other job, he was nice enough to make room for me on the staff."

"That's great." Maria smiled, trying to turn the conversation cheerful. "I'm so grateful there was a place here when I got to Ashland."

"There didn't used to be," Annette remarked, and then her face fell. "Oh, I'm sorry. I shouldn't tell you about that."

"About what?"

She shrugged uncomfortably. "Well, the reason there was an opening when you arrived is because Benny—he worked here before you—disappeared."

Maria took in this new mystery of what she'd thought was a sleepy little town with cheap rent and few selling points for tourism. "What do you mean?"

"No one really understands it," Annette told her. "He was here one day, gone the next, without so much as a trace."

"But, I mean, somebody must be looking for him."

"As far as I know, Benny didn't have any family. We were all the friends he had. That's why Gillian's a little cranky sometimes, you know. They were really close."

"Wow, that's...a lot." Another thought occurred to Maria. "Could Benny hear it?"

Annette looked up through her oversized plastic-framed glasses, which Maria was sure she'd had since the seventies. "No. Benny said he never heard a thing."

*   *   *

"You know, you're making more work for me."

It was closing time. Maria was getting ready to trail out behind José and Gill, with whom she'd made dinner plans, when Shirley approached. The door to the employee exit shut, and for the moment, Maria was alone with her least favorite coworker.

She'd been revising the newsletter for the better part of two weeks. Shirley had continued to criticize her work, although Maria didn't know how perfect a local library newsletter needed to be, ultimately. She was wondering if this was just a way to keep her feeling like the new guy, like she wasn't really part of the team.

It was starting to wear on her last nerve.

"Shirley, I'm sorry," she said, throwing up her hands, "but I'm trying as hard as I can. Is there maybe a reason you don't like what I'm writing?"

Shirley's eyes narrowed almost imperceptibly. "Like what?"

"I don't know—I'm new and you're not used to me." In her longing to catch up with Gillian and José, she remembered that Gill hadn't liked her much at first for a specific reason. "Or did Benny work on the newsletter with you? Is that what this is about?"

Shirley took a step back when Maria said Benny's name. That must be it: she'd been fond of him, and Maria was rubbing in the loss of him simply by existing. And for the first time, she felt a sense of something human in relation to Shirley.

"What do you know about Benny?" the other woman whispered. Benny's name came out of her mouth a low hiss.

"Not much," Maria admitted, trying to make her voice kind, "except that everyone liked him. Look, I'm not trying to replace anybody. I can respect that you miss him. And I'm really, really sorry you lost him."

Shirley continued to stare, her face unreadable as always. It was even more disconcerting without her usual placid smile.

"I'm going to head out," Maria continued. She felt truly bad she'd dredged up some rough memories, but that fact didn't make her like Shirley any better. "Maybe we can talk about the newsletter tomorrow? I really do want to get it right."

Finally, Shirley nodded. "Yes. We can discuss it later."

Gillian and José were waiting in the parking lot.

"Everything okay?" Gill asked.

"Yeah, just had to talk with Shirley about something." Maria didn't want to blab about how upset she'd left Mitch's second-in-command when they were still within earshot.

"Better you than me," José quipped. "Want me to drive? You both can leave your cars here until after we're done eating."

They hit up a local diner that didn't close until midnight. The library stayed open later than most restaurants in town, so there weren't many options to choose from. Thankfully, the diner was a good one—the booths were cozy, the food was delicious, and the servers were friendly.

"What's your deal with Shirley?" Maria asked José after they'd placed their orders. "That whole 'better me than you' thing you said before."

He sighed. "Shirley can be intense."

"How?"

"She kind of fixates on people sometimes," Gillian said. "You know, she decides that she has her new project or whatever, and doesn't let up until that person, well..."

"Gill, we don't know that's what happened," José interjected, frowning.

"What are you talking about?" Maria asked, and when they didn't answer right away, she took a chance. "Is this about Benny?"

"So you've heard about him," José said.

She looked down. "It's hard not to hear about the person whose job you took."

The server came with their food, interrupting the heaviness. Once Maria's burger and fries were set in front of her, Gillian caught her gaze.

"You know, I don't blame you for taking the job," she said. "I'm sorry if I wasn't so nice on your first day. It's just...hard. I miss him a lot."

"I'm sorry," Maria replied, not for the first time that night. "You said he was Shirley's project or something?"

Gillian's eyes hardened. "She used to make him rewrite every single thing. She said it would be good for him—that if he learned how to do it, he could take over the newsletter or whatever. Of course, she drove him away before that could ever happen."

José sighed. "We don't know what happened to Benny. He could've left town for some other reason, or...something might have gone wrong."

"In Ashland?" Gillian gave him a look of disgust. "We're not exactly the home of serial murderers and kidnappers, José."

"Hey, it's a weird place. Benny's not the first person to suddenly vanish from here."

"It's a dull little town," Gillian countered. "People pass through; not everyone's going to stay here forever."

"I know, but that doesn't mean that Shirley—"

"Shirley had Benny going to her place at night, after the library closed," Gill cut him off. "She made him work under so much scrutiny, he was going nuts! Of course she drove him away."

Maria thought about this. If Shirley really had contributed to Benny's disappearance somehow, it would explain why she'd looked so stricken when his name had come up. There she was, doing the same thing with Maria—being really intense, making her rewrite and rewrite. Was it because she wanted Maria to take over eventually? Her mind reeled with possible reasons for that kind of interest. Maybe Shirley wanted to retire early. Maybe she was trying to leave Ashland herself. Maybe she was sick and didn't have much time left, or maybe she wanted a prodigy, someone she could be proud of.

Maria didn't know much about Benny, but it seemed like he hadn't known how to draw boundaries. If Shirley wanted to take her under her wing but was too intense to know how to do that appropriately, Maria figured she could fix the situation. She could make it clear that she wouldn't put up with certain kinds of pressure, but that she was willing to work hard nevertheless. Maybe she could help Shirley attain her newsletter successor, after all.

"So, what is there to do around here other than eat?" she asked, wanting to change the subject for Gill's sake, especially.

The two of them barked out laughter. "I mean, I hope you've got a good internet provider," José said, "because there's not much."

"Yeah, you could always shop at the three competing boutiques in town, or go to the bookstore or the movie theater," Gill told her. "Other than that, like I said before: Ashland's pretty dead."

"What about the woods?" Maria asked. "Are there trails to walk through?"

"Sure." José shrugged. "The woods can be nice, and the docks are pretty, too. Just make sure you go during the daytime if you decide to visit places like that. Most people stay home at night, and you don't want to walk around desolate areas by yourself."

"Noted," she said, biting into her burger.

*   *   *

The next day, Shirley was conspicuously absent from work.

"I don't think Shirley's missed more than a few days since I started working here," Annette remarked as they put out supplies for a craft program coming up that afternoon. "Mitch always has to force her to take her vacation time."

"Maybe she's sick?" Maria offered, though she didn't sound convincing.

Annette shrugged. "She seemed fine yesterday."

Yesterday, Maria thought: the day she had brought up Benny and obviously upset Shirley. Could she be so distraught that she hadn't been able to come to work?

Maria's shift went until three that afternoon, so she figured she might be able to throw together some kind of baked good and bring it to Shirley that evening with an apology. During her break, she knocked on Mitch's door.

"Maria! How are things going?"

"Great, thanks."

"No issues with work at all? Everything with our patrons going smoothly?"

"Everything's great," she repeated. She was there on a mission, not to make small talk, but it seemed Mitch didn't get out of his office much and was happy for some company.

"By the way, I wanted to thank you, Maria."

"For what?"

He lowered his voice. "I heard how kind you've been to everyone, especially Annette. I'm sure you've learned about her...condition?"

"I know she hears the hum."

Mitch winced and glanced around, though they were clearly the only two people in his office. Maria wondered if he adhered to that kind of superstition where people feared mentioning a thing might somehow make the thing worse. "Well, it's not easy for anyone in Ashland who...experiences it. And with you being a newcomer, it's nice to know you're so accepting."

Maria shrugged. "It doesn't hurt me in any way. I'm just sorry that Annette has to deal with it. She's a really great person."

"She is that."

An awkward silence seemed inevitable, so Maria plunged forth with why she'd gone into Mitch's office in the first place. "Since I am new here, I was wondering: do we have a staff directory?" Mitch's jaw slackened in surprise, and she added quickly, "I have people's numbers, of course. It's just something we had at my old job. I thought I'd ask."

"Of course!" Mitch flung open a drawer and began flipping through file folders. "You'll have to forgive me. I should have gotten your information and had Shirley update this old thing. It's one of those tasks I usually let slip until she reminds me herself."

She nodded as he handed her a sheet of paper. "Should I just ask Shirley to add my information when she comes back?"

"That sounds like a plan! She'll be in tomorrow, I have no doubt. Our Shirley couldn't keep herself away if she wanted to."

As Maria turned to leave, she glanced over the directory and murmured without thinking, "Oh, wow, Benny's still on here?"

Mitch cleared his throat. Maria realized she'd have to be a lot more careful if she wanted to avoid the strange turns in conversation that seemed to plague the Glass Library's director, made that much more uncomfortable by how silent the building was. She could practically taste the awkwardness.

"I suppose you've heard about Benny, then. I...well, I'm sorry you had to learn about that. It's all still such a sad...situation."

Maria nodded, figuring silence might be the best policy if she wanted to get out of there in time to help Annette with the craft program.

"I hope hearing news of his...of Benny, well, hasn't put you off living in Ashland."

She was actually a little floored by this. It hadn't ever occurred to her that she might leave, not because someone who had the job before her had mysteriously left town. "Are you trying to tell me something about my job, Mitch? That it's...cursed, or something?"

The joke was as flat as Mitch's laugh in response to it. "No, no, of course not! No, nothing like that."

"Okay, then, I guess I'll get back to it." And Maria left the office as quickly as politeness would allow.

She was glad the directory listed home addresses as well as emails and phone numbers, otherwise the entire exchange she'd just endured would have proven worthless. Shirley lived in a part of town she wasn't familiar with, but so did everyone else on the list—she wasn't really familiar with anything yet. She'd have to let her phone do the navigating, for the time being.

"Ready for the craft?" Annette approached with a smile, but Maria could see she looked a little drawn.

"Um...is it bad today?" she asked gently.

"You noticed. Yeah, some days are worse than others. It's been really loud since about an hour after we closed last night. It hasn't been this bad in a while."

"I'm sorry," Maria told her. "Does anyone have any idea why it fluctuates like that?"

Annette shook her head. "I won't leave home tonight. Bad things always happen when it's this loud."

"Like what?"

Annette shrugged. "Last time I can remember it being like this, Benny disappeared."

*   *   *

Her plan had been to head to Shirley's before it got late, for two reasons: she still didn't know Ashland all that well and was more likely to get lost after dark, and she couldn't shake the eeriness she'd felt after speaking with Annette about Benny's disappearance and the hum.

But Maria was used to things not going as planned and wasn't surprised when her baking skills turned out to be even rustier than her interview skills. The half-hour brownies she'd intended turned into a two-and-a-half-hour kitchen catastrophe, but in the end, she had a steaming tray of rich, dark chocolate apology squares.

She referenced the directory Mitch had given her and plugged Shirley's home address into her phone. Frowning, she realized it was near the docks, one of the places José had warned her not to visit alone at night.

"I won't be alone," she reminded herself as she started the car, the comforting smell of brownies filling the air. "I'll be at Shirley's place."

The docks were expansive alongside the two-lane road with not so many boats as stretches of planked wooden walkways, wrought iron benches, and old-fashioned lampposts casting echoes of light across the slowly stirring waves. For such a small town, Ashland continually surprised Maria with how its structures, like the library and the docks, were impressive amidst an otherwise nondescript community. Maybe that had something to do with the hum and its effect on people, she thought—a kind of overcompensation for an unexplainable mass affliction.

There weren't many buildings to be found, and Maria started to wonder whether she was in the right place. Finally, the GPS brought her to a stop outside of what looked like a vacant warehouse. Tucked next to it, so slender she almost missed it, was the face of a narrow building that must house one or two apartments. The number above the main door matched the street address listed for Shirley.

As she got out of the car, Maria was aware she could see no one in the vicinity, hear nothing for ages. A light evening fog had spread up from the water, but it wasn't so thick that she could not see how very alone she was. She hurried with the brownies to the front door of the building, her sneakers hushing the sound of her steps as she moved.

She looked for a bell and couldn't find one. Feeling anxious to be inside and in the company of someone else, even someone she disliked as much as Shirley, Maria raised her knuckles and rapped on the door.

Silence. She knocked again.

"Maria? Is that you?"

Shirley's voice came from above; though the windows of the building were dark, Maria assumed that must be where her coworker was.

"Yes, it's me," she called, wondering at how flat her voice sounded. There was no echo, no depth to her words. "I have something for you."

There was a pause, and then she heard Shirley say, "Why don't you come around to the side entrance? The front of the place is a mess."

At this point, she'd do anything to get away from the desolate doorstep of the building. Maria walked around and found that the side of the building was in an alley even more desolate than its front.

"Great," she muttered, half-jogging to get to the door that was so far down the alley, it might as well have been around the back of the building.

The door remained shut, and a deepening feeling of worry filled the pit of Maria's stomach. What was it about this place? What was it about this night? She strained to hear the hum once again, thinking of Annette's warning about when it sounded louder than usual.

"I can't hear a damned thing." She wondered why it was taking Shirley so long to get to the door. She must have stood there for several minutes, her palms sweating from the warmth of the brownies, fog curling around the edges of the alley.

Suddenly, the door swung open. There was Shirley, an uncharacteristic look on her face. If Maria didn't know better, she'd say the woman was giddy.

"Um, look, I know I might have upset you yesterday, bringing Benny up like that," she began.

Shirley was also unusually silent. She just kept grinning at Maria, like she'd brought her something incredibly exciting.

"Anyway, I thought that might be why you didn't come into work today," Maria went on. Her discomfort was growing by the second. Something instinctive in her was screaming for her to get the hell out of there, and she wanted to push past Shirley into whatever room was behind her; it was dark and Maria couldn't tell whether it was a hallway or an apartment, but that didn't matter. "So, I brought you a little something sweet," she finished, the words pouring forth in a breathless rush.

Now Shirley's eyebrows raised as she noticed the tray of brownies for the first time, and she actually giggled. "Something to eat?"

"Yeah," Maria said. "Hey, do you think I can come inside? I don't know why, but I'm feeling a little faint."

But instead of welcoming her into the building, Shirley stepped out, pulling the door firmly shut behind her. "Why would we go inside when all the fun is going to happen out here?"

"The fun?" Maria took a step back. Her feet knew that something was wrong; her body knew it. Why couldn't she get her brain to focus less on manners and take her back home?

"Well, you brought a snack for me," Shirley continued, her voice syrupy sweet in tones Maria had definitely not heard before, "which is so considerate, given I wasn't planning on having anything myself. I mean, we didn't even expect you for days. We've barely had time to prepare!"

"We? Who else is here, Shirley?" Maria tried to keep her voice steady. It sounded so strange, like someone was holding a cloth over her mouth.

"My family," Shirley smiled. "Well, my true family. First, they took my parents and my sister—that was years ago. And then others, like Benny. Why, they enjoyed him so much, I knew I had to bring them someone new, but of course I didn't realize you'd be hired so soon. And I *certainly* didn't expect you here tonight, though it's a lovely surprise for us all." And she laughed again.

"I think I should go."

"But you haven't even met them yet." Shirley's eyes were cold as stone. "And they're so excited you're here. Can't you hear them, Maria?"

Maria shook her head, backing away from Shirley more.

"Benny couldn't either. Some of us can hear it, and some of us, well," that awful laugh, "some of us are too tasty for all that." And she raised her cold eyes.

Maria followed Shirley's gaze, tracing up the black-painted beams of fire escapes and drainpipes that had been fixed to the bricks along the side of the building. And from the roof, along those railings and pipes, stood several gargantuan arachnids, their faces pointed down towards *her*, their gleaming black eyes fixed on *her*, their horrible long legs like the poles of street signs propelling them down, down, down.

Their jaws moved, and Maria knew they were chattering and clicking, that they had been since she'd arrived. But she couldn't hear them. She couldn't hear *anything*. Aside from her own muted breathing, aside from Shirley's maniacal giggles, there was nothing, *nothing* as the great brutes came down towards her.

She had moments; the alley was long. There were several, maybe even more on the roof that she could not see.

"You won't make it," Shirley called gleefully as Maria turned back to face the way she'd come and began to run. "You won't even hear them coming, after all."

Segmented glistening bodies tore across brick and steel, jaws slavering, impossible legs pounding along the walls and pavement of the alley. Maria felt the vibrations closing in on her as she pushed her own legs forward, horror creeping up from the ground into her feet, into her scrambling legs.

But her ears were full of nothing, nothing, nothing but the silence that was, she realized, the hum of which she'd heard.

Reflections

If you gaze into the tree line long enough, you know you will see something moving there; that should get you through the next week, at least. Because if there is movement in the trees, it means she can't possibly be gone forever. If you just could find something—anything—out there, then logic says you might find her, as well.

This is how the days have passed since your sister went missing: alienating, slow, and oddly hopeful. Every moment a held breath, each day an extended pause as people look at you, pity and the puzzle you present mingling in their reflective eyes. You could see your own face there, if you looked back at them. Not an answer or a comfort, but a familiar face, as familiar as hers would be if—no, when she returns to you.

She disappeared on the coldest day. It hadn't been windy, but freezing and bleak, as if to warn you that soon you'd be living in a suspended state, waiting and waiting for a sister no one believed would ever return.

You have taken to standing out behind the house and looking into the trees where you played when you were children. You hear her giggle, not the womanly laugh that lives in her throat now, but the sound of her as you danced and tumbled through poplars, thinking only of play. It wrapped itself around you both, the magic of girlhood, that sensation of being always on the edge of something, as though you'd left infancy for a precipice on which you have been balancing since. You balance still, just as you have held your own heart tightly since the day she left, poised and not at all ready for a fall.

On this particular day, you bring an extra sweater out with you, reasoning that if she were to come back through those trees, she would be glad of something warm in the arms of the person waiting for her. The wool feels heavy in your hands and you almost regret bringing it, but for the hope that the trees will move and she will reappear.

Suddenly, the unwelcome memory of a dream from years ago: your sister standing before you on a surface like glass. You realize it is a mirror, that you are treading on an endless desert of mirror. For no good reason, the mirror beneath your sister's feet turns soft, and she begins to descend. The stuff is like quicksand, and though you reach for her, though she tries to pull herself up, the descent is too strong for either of you to resist. You lose her and wake.

Only now, as you think back on this night that robbed you of sleep and left you shivering until the sun appeared in the sky, you are not dreaming. Your sister has disappeared, and you are waiting to see what will happen, to learn whether she will return or you will also vanish and perhaps find her when you do.

Vision

Tom Hilton, divorce lawyer and widower, chose a corner unit on the tenth and topmost floor of the VISION apartment building as a new home for himself and his two children. He had not done much in the way of legwork when selecting the apartment. They were moving from another city, and Tom worked steadily and maintained that he didn't have the time or the inclination to visit the place he would bring his family to live. He merely saw there were openings in a luxury building that fit his tastes and his income, then made a series of phone calls to arrange a move.

VISION was not pet-friendly. It did not accommodate smokers, did not suffer late-night noisemakers, and while not policy so much as an attitude of the place, it didn't tolerate young children. The apartments inside were so white and polished that they did not fill quickly; from the perspective of many who came to view the space, there was something off-putting about it that they could not name. VISION was all sharp angles and crisp lighting, its windows floor-to-ceiling, its symmetry perfect. It was made almost entirely of titanium, glass, and hard white plastic. The thin white carpets that extended down long, mirror-lined halls were so immaculate and soft that, had anyone wanted to walk barefoot along them, they likely would have felt more liquid than fabric. Of course, no one would do such a thing.

Elana Hilton was fifteen years old. Her primary concerns in life were the number of subscribers for her livestream channel and what content she might be able to produce in order to make that number grow. Her brother Michael was seventeen and determined to be a tax accountant. He was decent at math and desired to attain a stable income and a wife who was better-looking than he felt he probably deserved, based upon his own appearance. Their father Tom might have noticed that his children had no great aspirations or passions in life, but he had become complacent in his habits after his wife had passed. And so Tom never realized that the hamster wheel of monotony he'd been casually walking had also ensnared his children.

It was unusual for a family to move into VISION. The people who found themselves drawn to apartments there tended to be seasoned in transience: a principal ballet dancer, an elite mural painter, a luxury summer resort manager. All worked without the steadiness of a twelve-month schedule at seasonal occupations with no dearth of unstructured time and no daily rhythm by which they'd set their lives. The staff who came to maintain the pristine quality of VISION were truly the most regular individuals to ever set foot inside of it, and although the building was massive and its cleanliness unmatched, these employees were few and far between.

The Hiltons' movers brought their boxed belongings on an afternoon while Tom was at work and his children both at their new high school. The broker had assured Tom that VISION was happy to supervise moves for busy tenants who could not be bothered to do so themselves, promising that there would not be any thefts or property damage. The movers were hired by VISION, and Tom paid for everything through the broker. When the family entered their new apartment, they found all of the boxes had been miraculously placed in the proper rooms, though none of them had done a particularly meticulous job in labeling them.

"Maybe they peeked inside the boxes they weren't sure about," Tom mused, beginning to unpack dishes onto a gleaming kitchen counter.

"They're still sealed with the tape we put on ourselves," Elana argued, looking at the neat stack of boxes in the living room.

"Saves us some bullshit," Michael remarked, to which Tom automatically and passionlessly replied, "Language."

Elana rolled her eyes. "Whatever. I need to go and do something to make my room look less like a refrigerator."

There was a bedroom for each of them. The children's were identical in size and scope, and shared a bathroom that sat coolly between the rooms, a door on each side by which to access it. Their bedrooms were so similar, in fact, that without the presence of the boxes containing their belongings, both Elana and Michael couldn't quite tell them apart.

Tom's room was the largest, with its own private bath to one side and a narrow adjacent room that might have been a spacious closet but for the small round window at one end of it.

The living room was large and open, connected to a full kitchen complete with dining space. There were also two spare rooms about the size of Elana and Michael's bedrooms. It had been decided that one would serve as a home office for Tom, and the other would be a guest room, though the family knew no one who might want to stay with them.

"Dinner's at seven," Tom told both his children before making his way into the office and shutting the door behind him.

Elana looked at her phone. "Three o'clock. Of course he's working for the next four hours."

"But now you have plenty of time to dress your room up for all your imaginary friends who watch your videos," Michael mocked his sister.

"Well," she returned, "we know you'll have enough time to jack off, but what are you going to do with the other three hours and fifty-eight minutes?"

With a rough shove at one another, the two parted ways and entered their respective bedrooms. After they'd left, the living room and kitchen were as muted as they had been before the family had entered. If not for the boxes, it would have seemed that no one lived there.

*   *   *

Michael grew bored of the new apartment quickly. To be fair, Michael grew bored of most things pretty quickly. He had few talents, fewer interests, and while his sister had been less than generous with her estimation of how long his new room might occupy his attention, she hadn't been far off the mark.

He stepped into the hall outside of the apartment. Because their father had chosen a corner unit, there was one door that faced theirs and a floor-to-ceiling window to the right, looking out on the manicured grounds of VISION and the less perfect world beyond. To the left, the long hall extended straight out, well-lit and with mirrored walls that had no visible seams to break up the reflections within them.

Michael's feet made no sound on the soft carpet as he started down the hall. Every ten feet or so, there was a new set of solid white doors facing one another. By the time he reached the opposite window, he'd counted eighteen doors, nine on each side. The only interruptions in this pattern had come in the center of the floor, where the elevator doors faced the entrance to an emergency stairwell.

The view from the window on the other side of the hall was so unremarkably similar to the one next to their apartment that Michael was sure he was going to risk entering the wrong apartment from time to time. As he was thinking this, smirking at the apartment on the opposite side and opposite end of the floor, its door suddenly opened.

A young woman, half a head taller than Michael, stepped out. Her hair was swept into a tidy ponytail that shone in the lights of the hall, such that it seemed to make her part of the space itself. She wore a matched sweat suit, all bright white, not a stain or a stray thread anywhere to be found.

She was exactly the type of woman Michael had long fantasized he would one day marry. She smiled at him, revealing a set of gleaming teeth worthy of a toothpaste commercial, if not rivaling the perfect symmetry of the hall itself.

"Hi," Michael said. He didn't elaborate or make an effort to be charming, something he had never bothered to learn to do. He'd never been noticed by girls at school, but had long ago decided that one day he would have a steady and solid enough income that how he engaged women wouldn't matter to his future prospects.

The woman didn't respond. She simply walked down the center of the hall until she reached the stairwell, then disappeared behind its smooth, white access door.

Michael was glad that whenever he did accidentally try the wrong apartment, it would be this woman's. Fleetingly, he wondered whether she always locked her front door. Then, with a noncommittal turn of his heel, he echoed her footsteps and returned to his new home.

*　　　*　　　*

Making her new room look less like a refrigerator, as Elana had put it, was proving more difficult than she'd expected. None of her belongings seemed to fit the place.

Its perfect lines and angles made her posters and wall art seem childish, and she tore everything down almost the moment she put it up.

She had a deadline she'd imposed upon herself for that evening, however the room might look. Elana took video deadlines extremely seriously: if she promised a video would go live at 6:oo, and then it was up at 6:15, how would that look? Who would even still be sticking around to see the video after that long? In those moments, she'd have lost her audience to a dozen other girls producing better content than she was.

She did her best using the floor-to-ceiling mirror on one end of her room. Just because she hadn't figured out how to make the room over didn't mean she couldn't look great. She made sure that her hair had just enough curl, that her lips wouldn't smudge color over her teeth, that her highlighter wouldn't betray a filter even under the filter she planned to use, which would be imperceptible if she did it just right.

Once she was ready, Elana shoved a box in front of her bedroom door, annoyed that the apartment had no locks within it. She'd have to convince her father to get a locksmith to fix that, property regulations be damned. She plopped down onto the white carpet, the mirror behind her and the phone strategically placed so that her pile of boxes was neatly stacked in the purview of the larger expanse of room reflected in the background.

"Well, here it is! I'm in the new place. Don't tell me it looks like I'm in some kind of giant freezer built to store torture victims—I already know that. I haven't decided how to make the room over yet. I'm just taking the day to like, get settled or whatever. Plus, Dad wants us to have family time tonight, which basically means eating whatever crappy food he's microwaved and staring at each other. Stupid, I know, but it's not like I have a choice. Well, that's it from me! See you tomorrow morning, when I will hopefully have some ideas of what to do with this place. I should be unpacked by then, at least. Later!"

She smiled coyly at the camera before killing the video, ran her filters, went through her usual tug of war between hating certain facial features and loving how she'd done her makeup and hair, then posted the video.

Elana started to unpack and her phone pinged once. It was probably her cousin Kelsey, who always liked her videos no matter what she posted. She ignored it and kept struggling with the box she'd taped a little too efficiently, until the phone pinged again. And again. And again. Curious, she picked it back up.

Wow, love the new place

Yo you live there?

Eerie

Awesome

You rich now or something?

Ellie hit me up, I'd love to visit

Her eyes widened at the barrage of messages. Never before had a video of hers attracted so much attention, never mind immediate attention.

"Maybe a refrigerator isn't the worst place to live," she murmured, glancing around the room and wondering how she could keep it looking as much like it already did once she'd unpacked all of her things. She could always throw stuff out, right?

*   *   *

Tom had no trouble setting up his office. Everything was where he'd remembered packing it, and the layout of the new apartment was more than convenient. He found that everything had a place, to the extent that it seemed the space had been meant for him all along.

The only item he had difficulty with was his favorite photograph of his late wife. Tom realized that the rules of VISION, which prohibited puncturing even the smallest of holes in the perfect white walls, would keep him from hanging the photograph, set in a frame with only a small loop in back and no arm to support it on a flat surface. He set it aside with his jacket, intending to take both into his new bedroom once he'd finished working. At worst, he reasoned, he might have to find a new frame.

Vivian Hilton, before she'd passed, had carried a spark of life that her daughter tried in vain to emulate and that her son would never bother to aim for. She had been the one lively and unique aspect of this family, raising them from the page of the narrative of their shared life and giving them a three-dimensional quality that without her, they sorely missed. Now, the three who remained were flat and bland, nondescript enough to blend into VISION in exactly the manner the building itself seemed to intend.

"I hope you like it here, love," Tom murmured to the photograph where it rested on his jacket.

Trapped in memory and beneath the frame's glass, Vivian said nothing in reply.

*   *   *

"What the..."

Michael looked down with disgust at the sizzling pieces of ham, shrunken and rank in the dish he'd used for the microwave.

"Way to go," his sister told him. "You'd better find a trophy wife who can cook if you can't even manage to use a microwave."

"I only put it in for two minutes," he shot back.

His father looked at the ruined meat and sighed. "You probably hit twenty minutes by mistake. There's no need to get upset, Michael—we've all done it at one time or other, and it's just a little leftover ham."

"I didn't hit twenty," his son protested. "And I think I would've noticed if the thing had been in there for twenty whole minutes!"

"All right, let's just settle down." Tom opened the refrigerator, then turned to his children with a rare but genuine smile. "How's pizza sound?"

"Okay, Dad, I don't hate new-apartment you," Elana told him.

"I put it in for two minutes," Michael grumbled as he dropped the microwaved dish and its burnt contents into the sink, but he obligingly followed his father and sister to the living room, where they got settled and Tom placed a delivery order.

Time seemed to pass strangely as they sat thumbing through their phones. A quiet that not one of them noticed took hold of the room; indeed, it had been there before they had ever arrived and promised, in its pervasiveness, to outlast the three of them. By the time the buzzer sounded, they all looked up in surprise as the sky outside the large windows stretched black and moonless over the city.

"Whoa, how is it night already?" Michael asked, sitting up.

"I'll get the pizza." Elana's face was drawn as she took the cash from her father. She was disturbed by the loss of time, and wanted something to snap her back to what felt like reality.

They ate in silence, and were again tucked into their own thoughts. At one point, hot oil burned Elana's hand as it dripped from the pizza. "Ow!" Sauce flew from the slice as it flopped back onto her plate and left two distinct marks on the white rug below. Nervously, she glanced over at her father.

"Don't worry about it," he said mildly. "I'm sure there's bleach somewhere in that box of kitchen cleaning supplies. I'll take care of it when we're done eating."

The family Hilton did not notice that they finished dinner at around one o'clock in the morning. They'd eaten lethargically, and except for Elana's mishap with the hot grease, uneventfully. The pizza was gone by the time they stood, and they bid each other goodnight, forgetting about how late the food had arrived and how much later they had been up eating, bite by bite, chewing slowly, digesting even as they continued to consume.

The next day, Elana would notice that the sauce was gone and assume her father had been the one to take care of it. She did not see the box of kitchen cleaning supplies still tucked underneath another box of pots and pans, both sealed and waiting to be unpacked.

*   *   *

During his first week of school, despite his underdeveloped social skills, Michael found himself approached by some of his new classmates. He chalked it up to the allure of someone new and figured it would fade soon enough, once they all realized there was nothing remarkable about him.

One boy, Smith, approached him after the last bell on Friday. "Hey, Hilton," he said. "Heard you live in that apartment complex, the one with the freaky name."

Michael hadn't really thought on the name of his new home, but he nodded. "Yeah."

Smith shrugged. "Want some company on the way there?"

Not used to having friends, Michael found himself surprisingly pleased by the offer. "Sure." He hesitated, then added, "You could stay for dinner, if you want. We've been having pretty decent takeout all week—none of us can seem to get the kitchen to work right."

Smith nodded, and together they headed for VISION.

As they entered the lobby, Smith shook his head. "Your dad's a lawyer, right?"

"Uh-huh."

"Must be nice, having all this."

Michael shrugged, uncomfortable. He didn't know whether to apologize or brag in this situation, so he just said nothing.

The elevator swiftly took them to the top floor, and as they stepped out, the woman from down the hall came out of the stairwell and turned towards her apartment. Michael noticed she was wearing the same white sweat suit.

He stumbled a little as he stepped away from the elevator and took a couple of steps in the direction of his apartment. His thoughts had lingered on the woman from the moment he'd first met her, and now faced with the reality of her in front of a new classmate, he was uncomfortable.

"Who the fuck's that?" Smith asked him, having recovered from his own less-than-subtle reaction to the woman.

"I don't know," Michael said honestly. "She lives at the other end of the hall."

"*That* lives down the hall from you?" Smith let out a low whistle. "I wouldn't have a social life either if I was around that kind of tight ass all day."

"She'll hear," Michael hissed, dismayed as Smith started to follow the woman down the hallway towards her apartment.

"Come on, Hilton, don't be such a pussy." He smirked over his shoulder and continued his pursuit.

Internally cursing himself for having invited Smith to dinner in the first place, Michael followed, trying to keep pace as his classmate came up behind the woman.

When she stopped in front of her front door and turned to open it, Smith deliberately collided with her. "Oh man, I'm so sorry, miss," he said. Michael saw him graze one of the woman's breasts with an open hand as he pretended to recover his balance. "I'm really sorry. I didn't mean to bump into you."

She looked at him evenly, that same pleasant, perfect smile she'd given Michael on the first day he'd encountered her set on her face. "That's all right," she told Smith in a voice sultry and soft as the fabric on her body and the rug beneath her feet. "Did you need something?"

"We'd love a glass of water, or even milk, if you have it," Smith said, his grin apparently irrepressible. Michael wanted to punch him.

The woman waited a beat, looking over at Michael expectantly. He should apologize for the jackass he'd brought into the building, he knew. He should explain that he was nothing like Smith, that he was respectable, somehow. He should demonstrate what an upstanding young man he was.

It probably would've been a lot easier to speak up if all those moments he'd put his hands down his pants over the course of the past week hadn't also been spent fantasizing about her.

In the end, he gave a sheepish shrug and a smile of apology. The woman's own smile stretched a little, and Michael found that at the edges of her mouth where her lips were joined were what seemed to be a few too many teeth. He blinked hard, thinking he'd imagined it; when his eyes were open again, the woman was pushing in her front door.

"Come in. I'm sure I have what you want inside."

Smith gave him a look like the two of them had just won a lottery they hadn't even bothered to enter. But Michael's pulse sounded in his ears as his mind counted those teeth: two—no, four incisors on top, four on bottom. One—no, two canines on either side, two on top, two on bottom.

Eighteen polished white doors, facing one another. Two white elevator doors slicing the air between them, facing a stairwell that went down, down, down.

"Aren't you coming, Michael?"

Her voice pulled at him and he opened his eyes— they'd been shut? He could hardly tell the difference, with the white walls when they were open and the white teeth when they were closed. But the woman was there, pulling down the white zipper of her sweatshirt, teeth separating on either side as she kept smiling and then turned to follow Smith into the apartment.

"Dude," Smith said, looking at him in incredulous glee, "*dude*, don't miss this! Are you crazy?"

Michael's gaze followed the two of them into the apartment, the woman's back now bare as her sweatshirt fell away.

The elevator doors slid open; he could hear them, slick as knives.

There was something wrong with her back and how she moved as she stepped towards Smith, who was eagerly and clumsily undoing his belt and jeans. Her shoulder blades were perfectly even, like two dusted moth wings fluttering in tandem as she moved. Each step was as long as the one that came before it, silent on the white carpet beneath her white sneakers.

The door to the stairwell banged shut, and Michael's heart was in his throat.

Smith seemed to take no notice of these sounds, of the fact that the door was still open as this woman walked half-naked towards him. All of those fever-dreams of mounting her, touching her, descended back upon Michael as he stared at a perfectly symmetrical back, as two identical hands began to push down a pair of white sweatpants and his heart seemed about to burst.

Animal instinct pushed forward in him, stronger than libido, stronger than the need to fit in, to not look weak in front of his peer.

Twenty visible teeth between stretched lips, and many, many more on either side.

Michael turned and ran, didn't stop running until his own apartment door slammed shut behind him, identical to its counterpart down the hall, which at the same moment also swung closed.

*   *   *

What's the bathroom like?

Elana had been fielding requests for the past week. People wanted to see more of the apartment and had started to specify what they were curious about. It was strange; she wasn't used to requests in her comments or direct messages, but she'd observed enough of the former on those accounts she'd long envied to know that most people weren't interested in architecture. At least, the kind of people Elana followed and wanted to be like and liked by weren't.

You wanna see the toilet? she responded, choosing emojis carefully so it would be clear she was gently teasing. She never wanted to offend anyone. How would she gain followers if she pissed people off?

The tub, the commenter replied. *You should take a selfie*.

It would not be the first time an adult man had made a suggestive, inappropriate remark to her on this platform. Indeed, of the few direct messages she did receive, a disappointing number were invitations for sex. There was also the one who'd offered to stab her. But she was surprised to see how many likes his comment had accumulated.

Should she take the selfie? It wasn't like she was going to get naked. And she had to admit, the tub was high and narrow, minimalist as the rest of the apartment, and it might make for a cool photo if she did it right.

Half an hour later, Elana had set the tripod and the timer on her phone's camera and put herself into the tub as requested. She chose a reclining pose, her legs crossed and arms lolling on either edge of the white basin. She'd narrowly avoided slipping on her own baby doll dress, the gauzy material too smooth for the sleek ceramic around her. She tried not to dwell on how cold and hard the tub felt, how it could crack her skull open with just one bad step, how red her blood would be as it slid down towards the steel drain.

The photo was the best one she'd ever taken; Elana knew it right away. She'd meant to give that kind of almost smile that famous painting had, but instead, her expression was distant. The light of the bathroom had left her eyes in shadow, such that it was impossible to tell whether or not she was looking into the camera. Her mouth was slack as her arms, and she looked lost, in a way. And with the faded pink of the dress and the stark white of the tub, she'd taken on a kind of pallor, as though she herself were fading, too.

Within ten minutes of posting, her follower count had doubled. And while it wasn't exactly an impressive count to begin with, it had been growing steadily all week long.

Thanks...She saw the preview of a direct message slide into her screen and realized that the guy who'd asked to see her in the tub had contacted her privately. Rolling her eyes and preparing one of the lines she regularly used on her brother, Elana opened the message.

Thanks for the photo. I'll look forward to your next one.

That was it. Nothing about wanting to fuck her or kill her, just a compliment. And, as she looked closer now, there was no way to tell if this was an old man talking to her, or even a man at all. The profile picture was from a movie, she realized, and the username was just a quote. This person could be anyone, and Elana did have to admit: she owed them. Their suggestion had doubled her follower count.

You're welcome, she finally messaged back. She waited, and although the person clearly read her response right away, they didn't say anything else.

Elana hadn't made any friends at her new school yet. She had barely spoken at all that week, and had been subject to side-eyes and curious glances that told her even in her efforts to do her makeup and hair right, to dress perfectly for any and every occasion, there was something about her that didn't quite make it.

It was nice to have someone to talk to.

*   *   *

Tom Hilton still hadn't unpacked his personal belongings. His office was set up completely; his bedroom, on the other hand, looked exactly like it had on the day they'd moved in, save for the stack of boxes, which were now neatly piled in the walk-in space that wasn't quite a closet with the little round window.

He was a man whose mind turned to function first, always, and so the state of the room didn't bother him. He had everything he needed to do his work and mind his family, or so he believed. But as the week came to a close, he figured the boxes had been there long enough and it was time to get rid of them.

Tom had also not yet found a place for the photograph of his wife, which he had placed on top of the boxes in the not-quite closet. As he walked in to retrieve the boxes, he found himself looking around, the sun from the round window revealing a space as neat and angular as the rest of the apartment. Then, Tom's eye was drawn to a spot on the wall perpendicular to the window.

There was a small, shining steel hook. It must be to hang a mirror, Tom reasoned, in what ought to be a closet. But then he realized it would also work perfectly for the photograph of his wife. He lifted the object and with great care hung it from the hook, on which it fit as though the two had been made for one another.

Vivian had always been the one to do the household decorating; Tom couldn't hang a painting on a wall for love or money. But as he regarded the photograph now, it seemed he had managed to set it exactly right.

"Look at you, my love," he murmured, smiling at the picture on the wall. "I'm sorry you can't be here with us."

Unpacking took Tom late into the night. It was the one complaint he had about the week they'd spent in their new home: he and his children seemed to lose track of time all too easily. He rationalized this as the effects of being in a new place, and he was not entirely wrong in that thought. VISION was indeed having an impact on how the Hiltons experienced time.

As he broke down a box and prepared to close the light and the space with the circular window up for the night, he heard what he thought was a whisper.

"Elana?" he called, turning around to view the empty bedroom at his back. His daughter was nowhere in sight.

Tom, don't leave me yet, the voice seemed to sigh.

He looked back to the picture on the wall, tensed in his late-night fatigue.

I miss you.

Tom Hilton was not a superstitious man, nor a man of faith. He was a skeptic in almost all things, a quality which had served him well in his profession. But inside every person there is the small possibility of hope for the impossible: a gambling win in a very bad year; a cure for a child's chronic ailment; an echo of a beloved spouse who has passed on. And whether it was the late hour or the new apartment or something else entirely, Tom suddenly found the small glimmer of possibility that lived within him.

"Vivian?"

I miss you, Tom.

He sank down to the floor of the space too large to be a closet and stared up at the photograph of his wife, an expanse of black sky adjacent to her smiling, frozen face within the frame.

"I miss you, too."

*   *   *

"You're not eating?" Elana frowned judgmentally at her older brother, who was staring wordlessly into his bowl of cereal.

Finally, Michael shrugged. "Not hungry."

Elana rolled her eyes. "You're so bizarre." It occurred to her that she should be concerned, especially when Michael didn't offer a comeback of any kind, just kept staring as the milk permeated the flakes in the white bowl on the table before him. But her phone pinged with a notification, and she swiped it open.

Their father came into the kitchen after both of them had been at the table for several minutes, which was unusual. Had either of them looked up, they would have noticed that his eyes had a sheen to them that had not been there the day before. As it was, Elana was preoccupied with her digital life, and Michael was reckoning with what had transpired in the apartment at the other end of the hall, which he could not make sense of no matter how he tried.

They ate in silence until Elana's phone pinged loudly and seemed to break what had been a kind of spell over them.

"Shit, class started ten minutes ago," Michael swore, standing up. "Why the fuck can't I ever get out of this place on time?"

"Language, Michael," Tom said, glancing down at his watch. "Though I can't disagree with you—my battery seems to have died."

"That's the watch Mom gave you, isn't it?" Elana frowned. "I thought you changed the battery right before we moved."

Tom nodded. "It's possible the guy I took it to gave me a dud by mistake. It could happen to anyone. I'll see about getting it changed again today."

Elana studied her father then, and an instinct within her said that there was something amiss. Perhaps it was a small remnant of her mother, something she'd inherited that was rooted in care and the impulse to worry. But as she opened her mouth to ask another question, one that might address both her father and her brother at once, her phone pinged a few dozen times.

Inevitably, she turned away from her family to focus on her followers.

"Okay, look alive, you two," Tom told his children, though there was little life in his own voice. "I'm heading into my office. I'm behind on calls, and I need to be out of here for client meetings within the hour."

Michael mumbled a goodbye as he left the apartment, eyes shadowed and downcast. Elana told her father, "I just need to pee before I leave."

Tom waved a farewell before taking his phone and coffee not to his home office, but into his bedroom.

The three doors shut at once: bedroom, bathroom, and apartment entrance. But as Michael made his way to the elevator, as Tom found himself turning into the space with his wife's photograph and Elana received yet another message from her anonymous friend, none of them were aware of the sound. It was a silent shutting, the soft white carpets of VISION muting any possibility of an echo that would connect the three sounds and the people who made them.

*   *   *

At school, Michael noticed there was an empty seat in his classes. He said nothing: asked no questions, heard no whispers, and kept his focus on getting through the day.

An assistant principal appeared during last period. She had two people with her: a plainclothes officer and what Michael guessed was a social worker. He'd had enough encounters with the latter after his mother had died to peg one on sight.

"All right, listen up, folks," their teacher called over the murmurs of the class. "We have some people here who need to talk to you, and it's important."

"Has anyone seen Smith in the past day?" the assistant principal asked.

More murmurs arose, as well as some worried looks on the faces of girls that Michael knew, even in the short time he'd been at the school, had no high regard for Smith. They reminded him of Elana in that moment, playacting for a group of followers and attention desperately longed for.

He said nothing still.

"If anyone knows anything," now the social worker spoke up, "we will be here after the last bell. You can come talk to us in the principal's office after class ends, and none of you will be in trouble."

"What happened to Smith?" one of the boys in the back of the room called out.

"We don't know anything for sure, son." The cop was speaking now. "There's no reason to panic—I'm sure you've all had a day where you might have wanted to skip classes, am I right?"

Some low chuckling. Michael noticed the cop looked more bored than concerned. He wondered what handcuffs could do, what a gun could do, against rows and rows of white teeth. He felt himself sweating, felt the hairs at the base of his neck pricking upwards, and drew one shallow breath after another. No one seemed to notice.

The adults had let the class fall into low chatter, and the teacher was anxiously asking questions of the cop and the social worker. She seemed the most concerned of all of them, though Michael overheard the cop saying something in response to her along the lines of, "If I had a dollar for every teen runaway…"

His hands started to shake, so he slid them under the desk. When the bell rang, he jumped, but he saw he wasn't the only one. Those same girls in his class were in a frenzy of upset over this boy they had never liked. Michael slid away, unnoticed.

The halls of his new school were long, technically much longer than those in VISION. But as he walked them, he realized everything felt faster and closer when he was away from those soft white carpets, those mirrored walls.

And if he knocked on the door at the other end of the hall from where his family resided now? Would he find Smith inside? Or had he been devoured by that silent, bright place where nothing was disturbed but everything disturbing, those halls that reflected and gave nothing back.

Michael walked as slowly as he could all the way back to VISION, but felt the entire way that it wasn't slowly enough. And when the white steps and glass doors to the lobby were facing him, he found the shaking in his hands had returned and only worsened as he made his way inside.

*   *   *

The family Hilton missed dinner that evening.

Tom was still in the small room with the round window by the time darkness fell. He reasoned it was because the clothes and other odds and ends he had in the boxes stacked there had yet to be unpacked. The fact that he barely managed to get through half of the topmost box did not seem to reach him, nor did the hunger he should have felt after not eating since breakfast that morning.

But Tom was smiling and whistling to himself as he stepped out of the space, and was more than a bit surprised to find his bedroom windows revealing a dark night sky. The small circular window next to his wife's picture had been outshone by the image and memory of the woman herself, to whom he had been murmuring as he unpacked the few items he'd gotten to.

He glanced down at his watch, forgetting it had stopped, and seemed to see in that small circle the reflection of Vivian's smiling face once more. He smiled back at it, and instead of checking on his children or making himself something to eat, he pulled back the covers and climbed into bed, hearing whispers as he drifted off to a dreamless sleep, the soothing promise of a voice he had loved and lost filling his ears and mind.

As for Elana, she had also never left VISION that day. When she received more messages from her ever-accumulating followers, she found herself taking photograph after photograph in the shared bathroom, most of them in the tub. She was frustrated she could not reproduce the quality of the shot that had gained such a positive response the day before, and finally messaged her new friend a few of her failed attempts.

It's because you look too lively, her friend told her.

I look too alive to you? She meant the message snappily, she reasoned with herself. It wasn't a sincere question.

You were so still in the other photograph. You looked like a perfect moment.

Elana was not used to the word "perfect" being thrown in her direction.

Okay. So what do I do?

It seemed to take her friend forever to respond. She listlessly checked post after post, reread comments on her own image she'd already looked at a dozen times, until finally, she was notified of a new message.

Practice.

"What does that mean?" she asked aloud, wrinkling her nose.

And, as though the person on the other end of the conversation had heard her speak aloud, she received a bit of explanation: *Practice slowing your breathing. Practice not moving.*

Practice until you get it right.

Elana climbed back into the tub, stretching out and slowing her breathing. The ceramic was cold beneath her, such that she was in no danger of falling asleep. But a kind of rest took hold of her as she lay there, staring up at a smooth, white ceiling, letting all thoughts fall away as she tried to be still beyond all else.

Night came, and Elana's body was still there in that tub, her limbs cold, her breathing shallow. Her phone had pinged many times since she'd begun her practice, but it seemed she could no longer hear it. All she knew was stillness, and finally, as dawn began to break, sleep that was undisturbed because no one had come to check on the girl in the narrow bathroom, motionless in a hard, white tub.

*   *   *

Michael's night was not so peaceful. When he finally walked through the doors of VISION and stepped into the elevator after his grudging trek from school, he found himself suddenly full of a kind of despair. It was a feeling of emptiness he hadn't thought about since his mother had died, but it suddenly overcame him, and as he considered getting back off of the elevator while the doors were still open, someone stepped inside with him.

It was the woman from down the hall. She gave him the same smile she had on the first day they'd met, no extra teeth visible as the doors of the elevator shut behind her.

Michael's hands began to shake much harder than they had during school that day.

After a muted moment in which neither of them moved, she matter-of-factly reached forward and pressed the button for the top floor of the building. There was no evidence that she had even noticed his tremors, or the fear that had wrapped itself around him completely.

The elevator moved silently upwards, but as the numbers shone on the panel above the buttons, Michael found he could not stand waiting beside such a terrifying presence. When they were halfway to the top floor, he reached forward and pressed the button for the next available stop, barely able to breathe.

Once the doors slid open, he practically fell out. He didn't dare look over his shoulder at the woman, just waited for the sound of the elevator doors shutting at his back before turning around. But the sound never came.

Michael slowly turned his head.

The elevator was empty, gaping open as though waiting for him. He looked frantically left and right, eyes cast down a hall that was identical to his own, to every hall in VISION. Uncertainly, he began to walk towards the open elevator. The woman had clearly gone, and it was still waiting...

But as Michael was about to step back in, the doors shut so quickly he was blown a pace back by the force of them. Had he leaned forward just an inch or two more, his face would've been crushed.

Ears ringing from the bang the doors had made, and sweating profusely now, he took another glance down either side of the hall. Turning around, he saw that the stairwell door was there, looking just the same as it did on his own floor. But behind the glass window that led to the white sets of stairs was a smiling face with too many teeth, gleaming and approaching fast.

Scrambling, Michael ran instinctively for the apartment that was several floors below his own. He did not know whether they would open the door to a strange boy running down the halls, neither he nor his reflection making a sound as he tore up a soft white carpet the color of bleached bones and shining teeth.

*   *   *

"Have you seen your brother?" Tom asked Elana in the morning.

She shook her head, eyes never lifting from the phone in her hand. There, in her photos app, Elana was swiping through picture after picture of herself in the tub. She looked perfect, though so cold and small that she again seemed to fade against the starkness of the bathroom and its angles, its ceramic hardness. Each photograph was more striking than the last, her eyelids softly closing her face so that only the perfection of deep slumber was there.

And it should have bothered her more, she knew, that she could not remember taking these pictures, nor could she account for how the angles from which they were shot might be possible with the limited equipment she possessed. It would have bothered her, but for the fact that she looked in these images so beyond what she had ever before thought possible, so striking and magnetic that she could barely believe this was her.

"Maybe he went to school early," Tom murmured into his coffee, which had already gone cold. He frowned at it. "I wish the microwave would work properly."

"It's Saturday," Elana said automatically at the mention of school. Her own breakfast lay untouched on the table before her.

Inexplicably, Tom looked down at his watch, which could not have shown him the day of the week even if it hadn't still been stopped. "So it is. Well, maybe he met up with some friends."

Elana did not reply with the snark she should have in regards to her brother's inability to converse with his peers. Instead, she opened up a new message from her friend who had told her to practice stillness until it was perfect.

How did it go?

She hesitated, wondering if she was doing the right thing, then sent along her favorite of the photographs that she could not account for having taken.

It's almost perfect.

Almost? she wrote back, emboldened by her persistent wonder at the image.

You should post it, don't get me wrong, her friend replied. *You'll get a lot of likes.*

But? Elana pressed, her eyes hungrily awaiting the next words.

You should try drawing a line down your arm or your neck with something sharp.

She felt herself grow cold, colder than she'd been in the tub. She wanted to reply with outrage, with anger, but she instead just stared as her friend continued typing, waiting to read what the next message would say.

Nothing that will really hurt you, of course. Just a thin line of blood, to make it look convincing.

Her ears seemed to ring, and there was a sense that she wanted to step back but couldn't, and the one making her step forward was herself. It reminded her of the fifth-grade trip she'd gone on, when all of the girls in school she wanted to be friends with were going to ride the upside-down rollercoaster, and it was the last thing Elana wanted to get on, but she needed to be friends with them. She had to be.

So she'd waited in line, had even gotten on first at the offer of a girl named Christie who told Elana how cool it would be to sit in the front car. Once Elana was strapped in, Christie said she just had to run and get a hair tie, that she'd be back in a second. And when a boy who was even older than her brother at the time was strapped into the seat next to her, she frantically turned and looked for Christie, only to find that she and the other girls had run off, leaving Elana locked in the only place she knew she did not want to be in that moment.

"Don't puke on me," the boy next to her said suspiciously. "I don't know why they let little kids on this thing."

She almost told him that she didn't know why they did either, and yes, she was very likely to puke, so didn't he want to call the ride attendant to let her off? But before she could speak, they were moving, and Elana had no choice but to endure.

In the end, she hadn't thrown up until afterwards, shaky legs getting her to the bathroom just in time. As she vomited disgusting amusement park food, much nastier on its second visit to her mouth, she thought that this was not Christie's fault, really. She had chosen to get on, she had chosen to prove how brave she was to the other girls, and she had been the one to survive the ride, not them.

Her phone pinged, and she saw it had grown dark as she'd considered her friend's advice. When she opened it, she found one last message: *Dead girls get more follows.*

And Elana knew, though her body screamed against such logic, that the point was sound. She began to think of her next shoot, and how she would get the blood to come forward just enough to make it look real.

"Well, I'd better get to it," Tom said, smiling absent-mindedly at his daughter. "Have a good day at school, sweetie."

He made straight for the bedroom. And as Elana stood and walked towards the bathroom, she called, "You too, Dad."

Both doors shut, and the apartment was silent once again, as still as the hall just outside.

*   *   *

Michael's pursuer had taken him all over the building. He had been running through the night, up and down the stairwell when she wasn't there, knocking on doors that never opened except when she was standing on the other side. When he finally reached his own floor, he did not recognize it. He was dizzy with fatigue and fear, and all he wanted was safety and a place to rest.

His face was nearly unrecognizable in the mirrored halls of VISION. He was pale and looked at once ill and younger than he was; the reflection was faintly familiar, he realized. He looked as he had on the day of his mother's funeral, drawn and sick, as though he would never be well again. Had he ever been well to begin with?

Michael pushed open the door of his apartment, and it swung inward without protest. He shut it firmly behind him after seeing that no one seemed to be inside.

The woman in the sweat suit might be just down the hall in her own apartment, and a delirium that had risen in him during the past hour made him chuckle at the thought. This place, with all its mirrors and light, it made you dance with yourself after a time, Michael thought. It put you in a box, just you and what you were afraid of, and it closed the door behind you.

He went for his sister's bedroom door before his own, longing to speak to her, for the sound of her snarky voice and the normalcy of a cutting remark. But Elana's room was empty, still undecorated, and Michael began to doubt the apartment he was in.

His father's office assured him he wasn't in the wrong place, until he saw that a fine layer of dust coated the desk and all the papers there. How long had it been since he'd spoken to his father? Michael couldn't recall. He turned from the office and headed for his father's room.

Once inside, there was no evidence of Tom. Everything was neatly put away: the bed made, the door to the walk-in space shut. Had he lingered a bit longer, Michael might have heard the sound of his father's voice, laughing and sobbing intermittently, responding to whispers from a woman who had been dead for many years and who did not reside in VISION at all. But instead, he made for his own room, hoping that, for some inexplicable reason, he would find his remaining family there.

Stepping into his bedroom, Michael found things as he must have left them: clothes tucked into drawers that were still half-open, a bed that wasn't made. He could not remember any of his actions from the day before. The week seemed a fragmented mess in his tired mind, and he rubbed his eyes, preparing to sink into bed once he'd safely barricaded the door and kept the woman out.

But as he blinked his eyes open once again, he found her suddenly there, sitting pertly on his bed, smiling toothily at him.

"No," he mumbled helplessly. "No, no, you can't be here, too..."

"Come here, Michael," she replied, and the sound was razor-sharp. He wanted to tear at his own ears. "You've been leading me around all night long. Isn't this what you wanted?"

Not daring to cross near the bed to get to the door of the room, he pushed into the shared bathroom and slammed the door behind him as quickly as he could.

When he turned to survey this new space, he found his sister in the tub, two long trails of red down each of her forearms, eyes glassily gazing up at the ceiling.

Michael's heart seemed to stop, then. Terrifying as his pursuer was—the fear he'd felt, the fatigue it had caused—all of it fell away at the sight of Elana lying dead in a cold, white coffin of a bathtub.

He sank to the floor opposite her, then jumped as the sound of Elana's phone camera going off echoed across the small bathroom. For the first time, Michael took in the sight of a tripod, the phone in its grip tilted down at the tub. After a stretch, the camera went off again.

He crawled to his sister and realized she was still breathing, though her chest moved slowly and the blood on either arm was real. Michael struggled with the jacket he'd been wearing, pulled it off and wound it tightly around one of Elana's arms, then grabbed a white towel from next to the sink and began to bandage the other.

"Come on," he told his sister through gritted teeth. "Come on, stay with me. Don't leave me, too."

Elana had not cut herself deeply; though her anonymous friend's advice about dead girls had resonated with her, she also wasn't ready to die and found she was much too squeamish to do more than make shallow slits along her arms. Her friend had said it only needed to *look* real, though of course what she hadn't realized was that sometimes we make things seem so real, we begin to believe them ourselves. And Elana had been practicing playing dead for so long and so diligently that now, she was finding it hard to leave her peaceful fog and rejoin the world of the living.

Her brother's pleas echoed faintly in her ears, and part of her mind urged her to wake from her stupor, to follow the sound. But there was another part of her that felt she was achieving some great truth, some art that was made of stillness and the biting fact that she still missed her mother every single day.

VISION was not a place that would rush a person away from the border of life and death. It recognized that such a decision took time and thought, and as much reflective quiet as possible. And it offered that same silence it had since the day the Hiltons had arrived, muting the sounds in the apartment such that Tom Hilton could not hear his son pleading with his daughter not to die, and neither child could hear their father conversing with the air that he believed held the loving whispers of his dead wife. Even Michael's calls for his sister were softened by the seamless white walls and floor of the bathroom, such that she remained hovering between those two critical states of being, still unsure of which to choose.

In the end, VISION was a place to reside, but its tenants would never call it a home. Homes are where families live, where individuals shut out the bustle of daily life and relax in comfort and the warmth of those they love, where being alone means leaving trouble behind rather than running from it all night along mirrored halls where one's footsteps make not a single sound.

Skin Deep

"There was a cut in the middle of her palm."

Are you sure?

They kept asking that. Did they think she was stupid? That she'd imagined everything? She knew the edges of her frayed patience were audible, but she was past caring about how she looked to other people.

She was alive, and almost hadn't been an hour ago.

"I'm sure. A cut, two inches long, in her left palm."

Someone put another blanket over her shoulders. No, not another; he was wrapping it back over her after she'd let it slip down. Her eyes managed to focus for a moment: so young, not a day over twenty, surely.

"I don't know whether to tell you to keep it."

What, miss? he wanted to know.

"Your kindness. Lord knows more people in your profession could use some, but I don't know if that wouldn't leave you a lamb among wolves."

The young deputy offered a confused expression that began as a smile then collapsed into a worried frown. She didn't see him after that; her eyes started drifting again.

Okay, that's enough, a new voice said. *You can ask her more questions after we've taken her to the hospital and the doctors have cleared her for visitors.*

She was helped to her feet, but was too dizzy to stay there. Once it was clear she wasn't going anywhere on her own, she was put onto a metal bed and lifted into an ambulance.

How funny, she thought. She'd been lifted not all that long ago, thrown on a wave and buoyed upwards before the wailing darkness had sucked her down and tried to steal her breath for good. And now, these men wanted to lift her up to safety so that they might eventually glean from her something not a one would understand in the end.

It was very funny, in the manner of funerals, death rites, the sinking of ships. What a shame she didn't have enough air in her lungs for a good laugh.

*   *   *

"Nayeli Hernandez?"

She looked up from the black coffee. She didn't know how long she'd been staring into it, trying to parse those dark waters where something had been pulling her down...But she realized the cup had grown cold in her hands, so she figured it had been awhile.

"Yes?"

"I'd like to talk with you about what happened."

She frowned at this gangly man seating himself across from her without invitation. "I'll bet you would."

"Please, I promise this won't take long."

"You know, I'm very good at detecting an empty promise," she told him. "And who said you could join this table?"

"Were you expecting someone?" He offered what he seemed to think was a charming smile, but Nayeli didn't charm easily, especially this week.

Her eyes narrowed. "Go away."

"Come on, I just have a few questions."

A light went on in her brain; how could she not have realized immediately? "You're a reporter."

"Guilty as charged."

"Okay, *definitely* go away."

"Look," he continued, not showing any signs of going anywhere, "you're the only one who has survived. Do you know how many bodies that thing has left in its wake?"

"I don't. Know or care, that is."

"Well, none, actually. Not one of them has been recovered."

"I fail to see how any of this is my problem," she said, starting to put on her jacket. If he wouldn't leave, she could.

He grabbed her hand, and Nayeli had a flash of a kind she hadn't since—since—

The reporter in front of her, shirt off, hair tousled. Her hands on his chest. A grin on his face, nothing like the opportunistic one he'd approached her with. Her heart beating fast, his pulse racing beneath her skin, and then the feeling of something between them, something cold and slick as water under her palms—

"Ms. Hernandez?" He was holding her forearms now, gently, steadying her as she rocked back and forth, her feet no longer supporting her.

"Oh, it's 'Ms. Hernandez' now, is it?" she replied, trying to appear much more in control of herself than she actually was.

"Please, let me help you sit," he said as he lowered her back into the chair. "And I'll get you some kind of pastry or something—it's the least I could do after I upset you like that. Uh, excuse me?"

As he was signaling the table server, Nayeli studied him. He certainly wasn't bad-looking; even her agitation at being caught unawares by a reporter couldn't have distracted her from that fact. And there was genuine remorse on his face, concern in his eyes.

"What's your name?" she asked. "You know mine already."

He nodded, having the decency to look a little sheepish. "I'm Chris." He offered her a hand, and she took it. "Christopher Herald."

"Herald? Seriously?"

The sheepish look morphed into a smile, the first genuine one she'd seen from him. "I know, I know—I'm literally a cliché. At least I don't report for *The Herald.*"

"No?"

"I'm with *The Daily Post.*"

She snorted. "Figures—they're the only ones who didn't make it to the scene. Playing catch-up for your boss?"

He ran a hand through his hair, and Nayeli recalled how he had looked in the light of her vision. She bit the side of her cheek to get herself back under control.

"I'm really sorry about how I approached you today," Chris said. "I was focused on the story, and I let myself forget I was going up to someone and asking her about a trauma that occurred less than a week ago."

This was an unusual approach for a reporter to take. "You're annoying," she told him. "But I don't think I hate you."

Chris laughed, and the sound was raspy to the point of being almost dry, blessedly so. "I'm glad I've met with some approval."

"I'm not giving you a headline, though."

"That's fair," he said, nodding. "How about this: would you help me work on the story? Acting purely as a consultant, of course."

"Of course," Nayeli scoffed, but she was curious enough to ask, "What would that entail?"

"Come to my office and take a look at the information I've gathered so far, then decide whether I'm close or way off with my assessment of it."

"It?"

"The monster."

It was such a strange word for what she'd encountered, and hearing it from Chris, there was a hollowness within her that almost seemed to ache, a pang of insistence that there was so much more to the whole thing than that.

"I'll come by," she agreed. "But I can almost already tell."

"Tell what?"

"That you've got it wrong."

*   *   *

She couldn't breathe; she couldn't breathe. She struggled, fought, pushed against, practically revolted, but nevertheless: she could not breathe.

Water was everywhere, pulling at her, dragging her, turning her into a thing that would strangle itself. It was beyond invasive; it went *through* her, rendered her something other than what she believed herself to be.

A thing that did not breathe, that did not need to breathe.

Nayeli gasped into the faint light of sunrise. Without missing a beat, she turned to the table where the anti-anxiety medication waited for her: two pills left, way at the bottom of the little orange bottle.

"Damn," she muttered, realizing for the first time how quickly she'd gone through the prescription. The town was small and people talked; she'd have to hold off requesting more and get through things the old-fashioned way.

Putting whiskey in her coffee seemed a little much even as she did it, but she had to pull herself together and head over to Chris's office somehow.

"You're early," he said, surprised.

"Your office is in a house," she replied, her expression demonstrating her reciprocal surprise.

Chris shrugged. "Well, I'm freelance. Comes with the territory."

"I thought you were with the *Post*." Now Nayeli crossed her arms, waiting for an explanation.

"I am," he assured her, "for this particular story, and for most of the stories I cover. But I still technically work as a freelancer, and I'm not worth cutting one of their precious cubicles in half—that office is busting at the seams as is. Come on inside. Do you want coffee?"

She wanted to argue further, insist that he'd been less than honest by sending her to his home, but he'd already turned around. And in fairness, the office was on the side of his home, with a separate entrance and everything—even a little kitchenette where Chris was minding a coffeepot.

"Sugar?" he asked.

"Lemon, lately," she said, looking around.

He opened a minifridge and retrieved a small dish with lemon slices on it. "I'm actually shocked this is in here. I must've made myself tea the other night and forgotten about it."

"How could you forget you made tea?"

Chris handed her a cup and gestured for her to sit. "You've never lost track of what you were doing?"

The comment wasn't uttered with malice, but it was enough to make Nayeli to lose her grip on the mug. It slammed onto the glass coffee table with a bang.

"Sorry," she muttered.

"Nothing to apologize for," Chris said with a smile as he sat across from her. "You didn't even spill."

"So," she said, looking at him, wanting to forget her moment of…whatever that had been.

"So."

"Aren't you going to show me everything you think you know?"

He nodded and reached for a file, then hesitated. "Do you think…I mean, I don't want to hand you anything that's going to be…I don't know…"

She sighed. "I will tell you if I'm not okay. In fact, we'll probably both know pretty immediately. Good enough?"

Chris gave her the file.

Nayeli began paging through, looking at the collected clippings and interview transcripts, all of them about sea monsters and what had to be dreams of the most eccentric town residents. Chris's handwriting, sketchy and light, filled the margins of most of the pages. She found herself brushing her fingertips against it, getting a sense of the man who'd made the marks: determined, driven, but kind, with a generous soul that came through whether or not he intended it, though most of the time, he did.

"Nayeli?"

She looked up. "Hmm?"

"I don't want to rush you or anything, but…well, you've been staring at that one marginal note for a good ten minutes now."

And so she had been. "Sorry."

"You apologize too much." That smile again.

She had to dig her nails into her palms for a minute as the image of Chris, shirtless and flushed, returned to her. But the sensation drew her back deeper into memory, back to the image of a woman's hands, sliced in the center of the palms, *both* palms, though she hadn't realized it at the time...

"Okay, you just went somewhere again like you did at the coffee shop," he told her, his voice bringing her back from that darkness, that fractured memory that at any given moment was gone as quickly as it was upon her. "Are you seeing anyone for the trauma?"

She laughed a little bitterly. "Where do you suggest I go in this town?"

"Hey, I know it's small, but there are a few good doctors around."

"Yes, and they very nicely made sure I hadn't drowned once I got to the hospital," she retorted. "There are some good MDs here, but no therapists worth writing home about."

"So," he said, seeming to understand this was a fight he'd lose, "what do you think? Am I as dead wrong as you assumed I was?"

"Most of these accounts are from other towns," she told him. "And a lot of them aren't all that recent."

"That's part of what I'm trying to show in my article," he replied. "The sea monster isn't from this town, but it is from around here. It's a recent transplant to our very local vicinity, but otherwise, it knows the area."

"If it's a sea monster," she challenged him, "then how is it able to move around so much? Some of the bodies of water mentioned are connected to rivers, but not all of them."

"I have a few ideas about that, too," he replied. "You saw in the Henderson interview, the victim's uncle recalled a strange man had come to town that month? And then, when I spoke to Angela Kwan, she mentioned her sister had the sensation of having sleepwalked each night during the week before she died."

"What do those have to do with each other?" Nayeli asked.

"Nothing, at first," Chris went on, an excited gleam in his eye. "But one of the specifics Angela told me was that her sister seemed to remember the presence of a man leading her back home whenever she did sleepwalk. He had dark hair and a deep voice."

"And?"

"And while old uncle Henderson didn't remember the man's name and hadn't ever met him, he recalled a deep voice and dark hair and eyes."

"So?"

"So, maybe this man is its keeper. Maybe he takes it from town to town, stopping in one place until it's done killing and then helping it move on to the next. Or maybe it's able to take human form, and this stranger is what it looks like when it's on land."

Nayeli was starting to feel faint. How was it that talking with this man about something she could not begin to explain had such a strong effect on her? "I think you're reaching," she managed, then took a slice of lemon and put it straight onto her tongue, hoping the sourness would help center her.

"I think you're shaken," he replied, observing her with the unblinking pensiveness he'd shown from the moment he'd sat across from her in the café. "Nayeli, whether you realize it or not, you know something. It's why you've been having difficulty talking with me about this since I've met you. Hell, I'd wager it's why you're sucking on an actual lemon now."

"I could just like lemons," she shot back, trying not to squint so much from the intense sour juices.

"Oh, yeah, that's totally clear from your face."

They both laughed at that, and the tension between them seemed to smooth itself.

"Isn't this kind of a big career risk for you to take?" she asked him. "I mean, from what I know about the *Post*, it's not exactly a conspiracy rag. What makes you think they'll print a story about a sea monster?"

He shrugged. "I sort of feel like, when life pushes at its own rules and limitations, journalists need to bend a little, too. My editors know I'm solid; I have enough reputable reporting under my belt to push a bit myself, although I probably won't be framing things in quite as direct a manner as I am with you."

"Ah," Nayeli said, "so I get to hear the term 'sea monster' thrown around because I'm not your editors or the reading public."

"You're a person who survived something my editors and most of the reading public will never encounter."

She nodded. What was there to say to that? And here she'd been thinking he might actually like her; silly Nayeli.

A burst of air left his lips, and he ran his hands through his hair. "Okay, I never do this, but—do you want to have dinner later? I mean, do you want to have dinner with me?"

Maybe she wasn't so silly after all. "Won't that get in the way of your journalistic ethics?" she teased. "Isn't dating a source a little taboo?"

"Well, you said it yourself: I'm doing a story on a sea monster," Chris replied. "My career's basically about to go down the toilet, anyway."

"One condition," she told him. "No sea monster talk at the table."

"It's a deal."

*   *   *

Nayeli had to go shopping. It wasn't a question; it was necessity. If she wanted to go on a date with this not-right-about-sea-monsters-but-still-great-looking   man, she needed something nice to wear. And there was nothing of the sort in the house she lived in, apparently.

She'd found an attic crawlspace. It was strange—one of the things she'd lost along the way was the memory of how she'd gotten here, how she'd ended up in this particular house. No one had come to give her clues quite yet: no landlord looking to collect rent, no mail about mortgage payments, not so much as a gas or water bill.

Up in the attic were fewer clues than she'd hoped to find, once it occurred to her to climb up there. She discovered no old boxes or storage that might explain how she'd come to be here. There was a bin with some scuba gear that looked pretty dated, but it was for a man larger than her, and she figured it was leftover hobby equipment that whoever had lived in this house previously had forgotten to take with them.

As Nayeli strolled through town, she found herself discovering each shop as though it were completely new to her. The feeling didn't bother her; she somehow sensed that she was accustomed to visiting new places. But in such a small town, she drew long, curious looks and whispers that were less than subtle. Sure, she was the girl who'd almost drowned the week before and people were bound to talk about that. But did they have to be so obvious?

Catching sight of a pair of earrings in an oddity shop that drew her interest, she stepped inside. The smell of old books overwhelmed her, and Nayeli saw that the walls on either side of the shop were filled top to bottom with leather bindings and yellowing pages. Throughout the floor between these two walls were tables full of mixed wares, such that she couldn't quite figure out a theme for the store other than "whatever it is, you might find it here."

The shopkeeper, an older woman who was organizing some trinkets over by the register, caught sight of her and looked surprised. "Well, bathtubs are clearly much too small for you."

Nayeli frowned. "Excuse me?"

The woman shook her head, dismissing her own remarks and stepping forward. "Can I help you with something, dear?"

"I was looking at the earrings in the window. The gold ones with the blue stones in them."

"Lapis lazuli," the shopkeeper told her, stepping forward to retrieve the earrings. "The stone brings clarity, but the wearer should mind that it's quite powerful."

"Thank you?"

The woman looked her up and down. "You're not wearing them with that."

"No."

"Then with what?"

Nayeli shrugged. "I haven't found a dress yet."

The shopkeeper sighed and gave a little eye roll. "I'm not at all surprised."

Was this woman planning to make a sale or did she intend to rude-comment all her customers away? But the shopkeeper gestured for Nayeli to follow her and she found herself just curious enough to do so.

The woman brought her to a table of what Nayeli had assumed were scarves folded into neat squares, but when her impolite hostess rifled through and found a white linen square she'd apparently been seeking, it unfurled to reveal a summer dress that Nayeli had to admit would look adorable on her.

"White's kind of bridal, though, isn't it?" she asked, still admiring the dress.

The woman held up a thick black belt. "Put this around the waist and wear a pair of black sandals: problem solved."

Nayeli laughed then. "All right, I think that should work. Can you ring me up?"

"You don't want to try everything on first?" The question was coy, almost as though the woman was testing her.

"I'm sure I can come back if there's a problem," Nayeli replied, equally coy.

The woman's smile told her she'd answered right, and while the exchange was odd, it was familiar in a way Nayeli could not at all put her finger on. She left the shop with the earrings, the belt, and the dress, along with a sense of comfort she had not felt in longer than she could say.

As she walked back towards the house, a strong wind came and with it, the smell of salt and a sudden spiraling darkness. The comforting feeling vanished, and she was left with a vision of black waters.

The wave came higher, higher, and it would surely drown her where she floated.

Then, the vision of that woman, eyes shrouded and face dripping wet, her palms split but not bleeding.

You've lost it, Nayeli seemed to hear the woman say. *You've lost it; now all is lost.*

A car horn honked lightly. "Are you lost, miss?" someone was calling.

Nayeli turned around to find a bewildered old couple staring at her from their car.

"Are you lost?" the woman repeated.

She shook her head, trying to muster a believable smile. "I just...I get migraines," she lied.

The old woman clicked her tongue. "Aspirin's the best thing for the head," she offered with a kind smile. "Two tablets and a tall glass of water."

Nayeli nodded. "Thank you."

Water was the last thing she needed, the thing that had almost killed her. And while the doctors had managed to drain it from her lungs, she could not seem to get it out of her head.

*   *   *

"You look...amazing."

Nayeli glanced up, startled, and found Chris staring down at her with his jaw slack enough for her to know that what he'd just said was the truth. She hadn't heard him approach, had once again been lost in thoughts she wished would leave her. But at the sight of him, handsome and freshly showered in a light gray jacket, she found she could finally focus on something other than the waters that troubled her mind.

"I have no complaints about you, either," she said, earning her a laugh as he settled himself across from her.

"I'm sorry I'm a little late. I got...caught up."

"Remember," she began in a warning tone, but Chris raised his hands.

"I promise, no talk of anything beginning with the letters 's' and 'm.'" As he said it, his eyes widened and he groaned heavily.

Nayeli burst out laughing. "That was too good!"

He grinned. "Well, if that's what it takes to make you laugh, I'll see what other horrible, accidental jokes I can think up this evening."

They talked about nothing; no deep forays into one another's pasts, no stories of bad dates or "you had to be there" anecdotes. Their conversation was perpetually in the present, full of remarks on the menu and what looked good, comments on the other couples dining around them and who seemed happy, and anything else that one of them might think to mention. It shouldn't have made for great conversation, but somehow, the two of them just clicked.

"Are you feeling like this is going better than, well, any other date you've ever had?" Chris asked as they shared a slice of cheesecake with coffee. "Or am I just enjoying my delusions over here and you're figuring you'll let me down easy after I'm stuffed with dessert?"

Nayeli laughed as she had done repeatedly throughout their meal. "No, no. I mean, yes!" She took a breath. "I mean: I'm having an absolutely wonderful time."

The wonderful time brought them late into the night until it was clear that they were the only two diners left in the restaurant. Nayeli realized she could have stayed there talking with Chris until dawn, beyond dawn, and she reflected on the strange sense of humor life so often seemed to have: of course she would find herself enthralled by a nosy reporter who was obsessed with sea monsters.

He dropped her at the house and though she didn't invite him in, she pressed a kiss against his mouth that said she would have liked to. Both dazed, they drifted their separate ways, the promise to meet again soon an invisible thread between them.

* * *

During the night, Nayeli rose from bed. Stepping into the chilling breeze did not wake her, nor did the cold, rough road beneath her bare feet. Her body trailed in a direction familiar and terrifying to her waking self, but in sleep, she moved without recognition of this path along which she walked.

The night air was harsh, and her hair whipped around her face. She'd fallen asleep in the white dress that she had bought hours before, though the belt and the earrings that had grounded her were gone. A car swerved to avoid her, the spray of debris from the road not waking her even as it peppered her bare legs. The driver was so confused that the instinct was not to hit the horn, but to drive quickly away from the apparition of a slowly walking woman wearing what looked like moonlight itself beneath a silent sky full of stars.

The river drew close as Nayeli continued on her way, and now her arms seemed to reach out for something, as though this were a search of some kind. There was a road that looked directly down onto the river, built high enough that even the heaviest rains could not raise the waters to the cars above. Soon enough, she was walking along that road; soon enough, she was at its edge, eyes still shut in slumber.

Her body teetered on the precipice, but then, a twist of fate: a hand on her forearm, strong despite its apparent age, enough to pull her back, enough to wake her.

Nayeli gasped, terrified by the strange but frighteningly familiar place where she'd never have expected to wake up when she'd climbed into restful sleep.

"Easy," the woman from the shop said, her grip still strong on Nayeli's arm. "Take it easy. Focus on your breathing, and you'll get your bearings soon enough."

"Where—how?" Nayeli gasped.

"One question at a time," the shopkeeper told her. "I can't keep up with more than that."

"What are you—what are *we* doing here?"

"Well, I was out for an evening walk, of sorts. I looked up and there you were, also walking, though it didn't quite seem like you knew it."

"I was sleepwalking?"

The woman nodded. "And while you were dressed quite nicely if I say so myself, I can't recommend the hour or the location."

Nayeli shook her head. "I've never done that before."

The woman raised an eyebrow, then finally let go of Nayeli's arm. "My dear, I get the sense that you've done a lot of things you're not aware of. At any rate, I suggest you head home, or at least back to wherever it is you came from."

She nodded, starting to shiver with cold and with the memory of that night when she'd had a much closer encounter with the river below.

"Will you be able to get there on your own?" the woman asked, her gaze never faltering.

"I will," Nayeli told her. "Thank you for...thank you."

Frowning, the woman said, "I'd take you facing things when you're awake as thanks, rather than this subconscious roulette you seem to be intent on playing with yourself. But it's your life, I suppose."

And she turned and walked in the opposite direction, down the road that would eventually lead to the banks of the river, leaving Nayeli shivering, confused, and alone with that sense of dread she had never quite managed to get rid of.

*   *   *

"What do you mean, you were sleepwalking?"

She rolled her eyes. "I knew I shouldn't tell you. You're making a big thing of it already."

"Nayeli," Chris said as he handed her a cup of tea, "you start with 'so I sleepwalked the other night' and I'm not supposed to react to that?"

Why was this sea monster conspiracy theorist suddenly so pragmatic? She was about to grumpily ask him as much when their gazes caught, and she found a smile on her face in spite of herself. "It isn't fair," she finally told him.

"What isn't?"

"You're unquestionably annoying, but I can't really get annoyed at you."

"What a relief!" he teased, settling down on the sofa next to her. "Now, talk to me. What's going on?"

She spoke about the night out by the river reluctantly, doing her best to downplay the whole thing, but Chris's face was full of concern.

"I've heard of extreme traumatic reactions before," he murmured after she'd finished. "But I don't know about sleepwalking to the scene of the traumatic event."

Nayeli shrugged. "Well, you know me—always have to be special in some way."

"You should stay here for a few nights," he said, then blushed as she raised an eyebrow at him. "I mean, not that we have to...I could always...this is such a great couch, I fall asleep on it all the time!"

"You're cute," she told him honestly.

Chris winced. "Yeah, that was not my finest moment."

Nayeli leaned in. "What makes you think I want you on the couch?"

He cleared his throat and turned towards her, sliding his hands onto hers. There was something about the gesture that felt especially intimate to Nayeli, though she couldn't tell what it was. The sensation of his fingertips lightly pressing into her palms made her feel as though they were somehow one unit already, one form that had only been temporarily separated into two. The back of her mind rose up at this thought, seemed to say she shouldn't lose it, should focus on the idea and sensation because there was something important contained within, but then their lips came together and Nayeli was lost in Chris, all other thoughts falling away.

"So you'll stay?" he asked when they finally broke apart.

"For tonight," she told him. "We can see what happens from there."

*   *   *

Nayeli arrived some hours later with a change of clothes and a toothbrush tucked into a small bag. While she was wearing simple joggers and a black tank, she'd put the earrings from the shop back on, wanting to generate at least a reminder of the glamour she'd donned the other night. She had nothing slinky in her drawers to wear and hoped that if they did sleep together, her naked self would be enough for Chris.

It wasn't like she had another skin to change into.

The thought was a strange one, occurring to her as she raised a hand to knock on the door. But Chris's smile at seeing her melted away any thoughts she had beyond the excitement that she'd be spending the night with someone who stirred things within her she hadn't known could be moved.

She followed him to the bedroom, which was simple as the one she'd been sleeping in. No art decorated the walls, no photos stood on the tops of dressers or the night table next to the full-sized bed. There was a slightly overfull basket of laundry in one corner, but beyond that, the room was neat and soothing in its simplicity.

"I thought we could get a pizza and watch some monster movies," he said as he pulled some folded towels from his closet and Nayeli unpacked what little she had brought.

"Monster movies?" she asked, putting a hand on her hip.

"Good old-fashioned land monsters," he promised, and they both laughed. "I was thinking mummies?"

"I could go for a mummy movie."

Afternoon quickly turned to evening, to dinner and their silly choice of movie, and then to bed, where Nayeli relived the flash of Chris she'd had on the day they had met. His hair was tousled as they kissed and peeled off one another's clothing, his face flushed, his eyes bright. And though that liquid coolness she recalled never came between them, there was something else, something so solid and soothing she might have held it in the palms of her hands: the feeling that this man would see her home, wherever that might turn out to be. The notion made her realize that she hadn't been living in a house that was her own, but Nayeli had always known that, on some level. And with Chris wrapped around her, it didn't matter in the slightest.

They fell asleep side by side, and both slept soundly until Nayeli rose as she had earlier that week and began walking out into the night. Again, the cold air on her bare skin did not wake her, and this time her route was different, though the destination was the same.

She stood on the edge of the river, past the high precipice off the road on which she'd been stopped by the shopkeeper, who was now nowhere in sight. And as she had previously, Nayeli began leaning dangerously towards water that was close, so much closer than it had been before.

Someone screamed her name into the night. Her eyelids fluttered open in confusion, and she found herself, naked in the cold, staring across from the specter of a woman rising from the river's churning waters, a woman that Nayeli had last seen on the day she'd almost died.

Her name echoed in her ears, and an instinctive fear kept her frozen in place. But the woman, impossible in how she hovered, how she emerged above the threatening liquid darkness below, seemed to make a sound of her own. Nayeli heard it in her mind, closer than the distant shouts ripped away by freezing winds.

Draped all in white, water pouring from her hair and eyes, the ghostly figure reached forward, an illuminated current in the darkness, and Nayeli felt herself hesitate, suddenly much more cognizant and able to think beyond instinct. The urge to run was quieted by a sense that she knew this person, this wraith who'd pulled her beneath the waves not so long ago.

The hands reached forward. The cuts within the palms were deep and bloodless, as though these wounds were meant to be, some deliberate stigmata that had written itself like words on this body, like she held portals to other worlds in her very hands. Her face was still vague, but even in the way she reached out, there was something uncanny, something neither alien nor extraordinary.

Nayeli couldn't grasp why the woman suddenly seemed so familiar. She was terrified, but there beyond her terror was the certainty that this was neither strange nor nameless spirit, that this woman was someone she'd known, someone she should know.

But, soon as the face began to form more clearly before her, the woman was gone and it was Chris screaming her name, pulling her back from the edge of the river which splashed roughly under the dark of night. He wrapped her first in his arms and then in the coat he wore, and her body seemed to allow itself to recognize the shock of the cold and the chill of the wind for the first time. She shivered uncontrollably.

"We have to figure this out," he told her, shaking a bit himself as he pressed his lips to her forehead. "Nayeli, you can't continue on like this."

He wasn't wrong, she knew. But what did that really mean?

*   *   *

Days later, Nayeli was sipping at the last of the morning coffee, paging through a book she'd found in Chris's office. He'd gone out to run errands, and she was trying to keep herself occupied—anything to distract her from the disturbing realities she could no longer ignore, no matter how much she wanted to.

Take the fact that she didn't seem to have a job. How had she been taking care of herself? Where did the money she had in the house she'd been living in come from? And where were her friends, and for that matter, her family? Did she have any?

Why couldn't she remember anything from before she had nearly died?

Chris had talked more about trauma and shock, but Nayeli had a nagging feeling that it was more than that. There was something she was missing, something critical she needed to know.

"We'll figure it out," he'd said, and Nayeli had noted that he had again included himself, as though this puzzle belonged to him as much as it did to her. It wasn't invasive, but comforting; she knew that Chris cared about her and didn't intend to abandon her, even if things got weird. And that was good, because they seemed to get weirder by the minute.

Growing bored of the book, she nonchalantly leaned back on the office sofa. A file caught her eye amidst the mess on the table. Unlike the others, this one was new: it had a crispness to it, sticking out slightly from beneath heaps of paper.

She didn't want to snoop, but what else was there to do while she waited for Chris to get back? Besides, it would just be something silly about sea monsters, she was sure. She tugged at it, and the file eventually came away from the mess and into her hands.

At first, Nayeli only saw the clippings that related to the accident: her name mentioned in a few, one with a picture of her by the water after they'd pulled her out. She felt strangely distant from these accounts of what had happened to her, this reporting that seemed so removed from the fear and darkness she associated with that night.

She was going to set the file aside—she didn't need to relive things through the eyes of people who didn't even know what had really occurred—but then an older clipping caught her eye:

Enrique Hernandez, 43, Killed in Car Accident

Her blood ran cold, her head seemed to swim. She heard a voice in the back of her mind: "You must hold on, mija. No hay cariño como el cariño de una madre. I need you to remember that, always."

Enrique Hernandez was her father, a father she had lost and forgotten until this moment. This wasn't a file about her accident; it was a file about her. Chris was researching her.

He returned to find her there on the sofa. The file was open on the table, though Nayeli hadn't been able to bring herself to go through it further.

"I can explain," he began, but Nayeli was already shaking with the anger she had only just realized was at the top of the emotional heap she was holding inside.

"How could you do this without telling me? Without asking me?"

He shook his head helplessly. "I thought I could help, I swear. I mean, you've been sleepwalking, and—"

"That doesn't give you permission to...to investigate me!" Tears filled her vision. "I'm not one of your assignments, Chris."

"Nayeli, I know that. And I—"

She stood abruptly and went for the office door.

"Wait, where are you going?" He rushed after her. "Nayeli, please: I should have told you and I am sorry, but you have to know I would never do anything to hurt you."

She hesitated at those words; there was something contained in them, something that felt like a glimmer of hope on a dark path through a labyrinthine wood.

"I just want to help you figure this out," he went on.

The light she'd caught seemed to dim. "I won't figure it out this way—not with you treating me like a subject who's part of your job."

"Please don't leave," he said, his voice cracking. "Nayeli, I'm afraid for you."

"I know." She sighed, pressed one hand against his cheek. "I'm going to find answers of my own. I'll come back to you if I manage to get any."

"What if you don't?"

She let the question hang and walked away.

*   *   *

The problem was, Nayeli didn't know where to look for those answers. She went back to the house she'd been living in, but nothing came to her. She wandered around town, and still, there was nothing for her to find.

It was a tiring and futile day. She lay back on the bed, thinking of her father and the fact that she hadn't remembered him until now. But as she began to slip into sleep, a wave seemed to sweep over her: she saw hands reaching out, a woman crying even as she hovered at the center of a maelstrom, and there was a feeling of something being taken from her, a sense of loss that could almost rip her in two...

With a sharp gasp, she sat up in bed, not allowing herself to fall asleep. "Enough is enough," she said aloud, and though she didn't quite know what she meant by it, she found herself slipping on a pair of sneakers and hurrying out of the house.

She jogged into town, forcing herself not to break into a run as she knew that the urgency she felt needed to be tempered with staying clear-headed. And she found herself turning up the street where the little oddity shop was located.

It was the middle of the night. Every business, even the bars and pharmacies, had closed until morning. But there, hanging outside of the shop, swinging gently in the wind, was a lantern, brightly shining against the dark. It was as though someone had known of her need and had kept the lights on, just in case.

When Nayeli knocked on the shop door, there was movement in the shadowy area behind the register, and then the older woman emerged. "You took longer than I'd thought you would."

"Thanks for waiting," Nayeli said, though she wasn't sure what they were talking about.

The shopkeeper beckoned her inside. Nayeli realized that despite the fact that the woman hadn't turned on any lights in the shop, it was far from dark. There were several pillar candles lit on many of the spare surfaces, and while those were few, enough light flickered from them to give the room shape and detail. Nayeli realized that the shop had a smell she hadn't noticed before: a gentle, warm incense that left in its wake afternotes of the ocean itself.

"Now what?" she asked a little helplessly.

The shopkeeper gestured to a space on the floor. "My advice? Ground yourself and take the time that you need, since you obviously haven't done so yet."

Nayeli sat down on the floor, fatigue preventing her from arguing or questioning further. She took a deep breath and tried to do as instructed, to ground herself on these wooden floorboards, solid and heavy as they supported her and everything around her. Nayeli shut her eyes and started to think on the night that had frightened her so badly; almost immediately, she felt herself swept up in dark waters. Her body tensed for a struggle.

The shopkeeper sighed. "If you're going to go about it that way, it's no wonder it's taking you forever." She walked past the register and opened a back door, which she shut firmly behind her, leaving Nayeli alone on the floor.

"What..." But the question left her before she could form it, and she understood that the woman had been right. *This is not the way,* Nayeli realized, shrugging her shoulders and shaking her head in an effort to release the tension. Something Chris had said resonated with her, as well. *There is no future if I keep fighting this way.*

So she stopped struggling and dove deep within herself. When the fear inevitably began to rise, she released it by facing it head on; she looked through panic and found clarity as her mind began allowing her to remember.

Her father had been sick. Something terminal, something that would take him from her no matter what. That was when she had started to lose it, to lose her grip on the half of herself that was missing now, the part that was still murky beneath waves of obscurity within her mind.

Then, there had been the accident. Nayeli had thought she would have more time with him, but she got the news and realized there would never have been time enough. Her father was all she'd had left, after...after...

Enrique Hernandez, 43 years old, leaves behind a 16-year-old daughter.

Suspected vehicular suicide.

Terminally ill man walks into the middle of the road on a dark night.

Once upon a time, a little girl lost everything and then she herself was lost...

Headlines and whispers echoed through her mind, and tears streamed down her cheeks, warm from the heat of her face and the candles burning brightly all around her. Nayeli took unsteady breaths, but did not open her eyes. She knew this was only the beginning, and she pushed further, pushed into the darkest depths of the memory that resisted her even now.

They had traveled from place to place. It was difficult for her father; he couldn't get the best medical care when they had to move so much, but they had no choice. He was doing his best to protect her, to help her get it under control, to get it back before someone made the connection.

"This is part of who you are," he had told her. "And as long as you hold onto yourself, she will never really leave you."

She will never leave. She is part of me.

But I lost her, Nayeli remembered, then said aloud: "Now all is lost."

"No." The shopkeeper had returned, was staring down at her from above the counter like a specter herself, shaking her head. "Not all."

"But she's gone, and I don't have it anymore." The tears flowed freely. "And when she came back, she tried to drown me."

The shopkeeper came around the counter and knelt on the floor in front of her. She gently took Nayeli's hands. "Is that really what happened?"

A flash of darkness, water rising, and Nayeli was brought back to that night. There was a quiet sound within the roaring waves that somehow reached her, a humming she had known long before she'd lost her way. It was a song, a lullaby, hers from the cradle and echoing in her memory now.

"You are very rare, my dear," the old woman told her softly. "Rare because that second skin of yours, the one you're missing, is inherited. It's something passed to the one its previous owner loves beyond all else, so much that she will give up her very skin and her life along with it."

Nayeli shook her head. "I didn't ask for that."

"Nevertheless, it was yours to keep and protect. We don't always get to choose the love we receive."

"But why is she here? Why is my mother back now? She died so many years ago."

"Whether or not you meant to, you've raised her spirit. She died so that you might thrive as she once did," the woman told her. "When you separated from that part of yourself, she felt it and assumed that without the skin, her child was lost."

"So now she drowns people?" It still didn't make sense.

"She has joined with the skin once more, and together, they are a formidable threat."

"No," Nayeli countered. "My mother was kind. She wouldn't hurt anyone."

The shopkeeper raised an eyebrow. "A mother who believes her child is lost? What won't she do?"

And that face, fearsome even as it was familiar, rose in her mind. There was a desperation in the arms draped in white ghostly fabric, hands reaching out with the slits that anchored the second skin, the skin that had protected Nayeli and helped her breathe steadily, even deep underwater, until she lost her father and had nothing left to love.

"You still have a few hours until dawn." The shopkeeper was standing by the door. "There is still time to act, though the longer that skin is separate from you, the greater the chance it will find someone else to pull under."

"But how?" she asked, rising unsteadily to her feet.

"If she thinks you're lost, prove her wrong." The woman tilted her head, considering Nayeli. "Make sure you believe it, though. If you're not convinced, she won't be, either."

*   *   *

She was back on the edge of the river, her breath coming in puffs of vapor that seemed in their rhythmic evenness to count the minutes themselves. This time, though, Nayeli was wide awake, waiting for the spirit of her mother and the second skin that she had shed in her grief.

As she'd walked from the shop to the river, the walls of her memory had continued to fall away. She remembered the sorrow she'd felt when she had first been given the skin. Her father had been there to remind her that this was the greatest show of love she might ever receive. He was there with her the first time she used it, anchored to her palms by slits identical to those her mother's hands had borne.

As long as you hold onto yourself, she will never really leave you.

Then, there had been the bliss of swimming deep into liquid darkness, to only surface every half hour or so while discovering the magic of a world below. Her father had frequently gone with her as he had once done with her mother, the scuba gear she'd found in the attic having belonged to him. And despite the grief Nayeli knew they both felt at her mother's death, there was a whole new joy they found swimming together. Beyond that, she was gifted visions that her mother had also had, a sight that was tied to the skin and allowed the seer access to past and future. Through it, Nayeli was able to learn her mother's childhood and young womanhood firsthand, witnessing so much that words could never have told her. This was something unique to her family, something precious that had passed to her, and by exploring life beneath the waves, she could learn this other world her mother had loved, retrace the dives and turns she'd made before Nayeli was even born.

"Come on," she whispered into the cold air, staring out across the dark waters. "Where are you?"

The night was so quiet, it almost scared her to speak into it. There was a sense that she was the only person in existence for as far as the eye could see and even beyond; it reminded her of the despair she'd felt at being left completely alone.

When her father had received his diagnosis, Nayeli had loosened her hold on the skin. She couldn't lose another part of her family without leaving part of herself behind, it seemed. And now she understood why they'd needed to move so much: she had started the drownings with her grief and reckless abandonment of the skin. It was the saddest, most furious part of herself, and left to its own devices, it had become the sea monster Chris had been hunting. They'd traveled to keep from being found out and connected to all of the deaths, but also because grief could not remain still. Her father tried in vain to reunite his daughter with her second skin, growing sicker by the day.

A sudden churning began out in the river, and Nayeli braced herself for what would come next.

Her mother's spirit rose slowly, and for the first time, Nayeli could see clearly how this shade was not the woman she'd known. Her eyes were deep and seemed not to grasp the world around them, even as water and tears dripped down her ghostly face. Those hands outstretched were grasping for a child that was nowhere to be found.

"I'm here!" Nayeli called, trying to catch the spirit's attention. The waves grew more wild, and the surface began to rise. Without her second skin, that gift from the mother who'd loved her, she knew she did not stand a chance in such waters. "I'm sorry I lost the skin, but I'm ready to take it back! No one else has to drown!"

Winds stole the words straight from her lips, and the shade of her mother did not respond. The ghost began wailing, and like a serpent, a dark shape much larger than the skin Nayeli had worn rose out of the waves below.

"Please!" she screamed, but the sound was nothing against the heartbroken wails and rising darkness. The waters came forward, and the dark snaking monster her skin had become seemed to see what her mother's ghost could not. It made for her.

"Mami, I'm right here," Nayeli whispered as the monster drew down to take her, tears of her own streaming from her eyes like echoes of those on her mother's face.

"Nayeli!"

By the time she realized someone was calling for her, Nayeli was already beneath the waves. As she had last time, she allowed fear to begin to take her. Then, she saw the glowing form of her mother's spirit studying her, gazing at her in sorrow, and she suddenly understood: her mother couldn't recognize her as long as she remained lost, separate from anything that might root her to this world. If only she could reach her, let her know that she was still here...

As Nayeli tried to signal her mother under the water, there was a sudden splash behind her, and she had to turn from the spirit to see what it was. Chris was swimming towards her, a strange mix of terror and determination on his face as he pushed against the wild currents.

Her heart lurched, and a scream ripped itself out of her as she saw the serpent turn its attention to this man, this body that had dared enter its domain. Forgetting about ghosts and a sad past, Nayeli allowed herself only one thought as she used her own expert limbs to propel herself towards Chris: *I can't lose you, too.*

As the darkness wrapped itself around him, Nayeli found she was able to catch hold of it. It fought her, but she used every ounce of her strength to pull it away from Chris, to make sure that this man who stirred parts of her no skin could ever quell or quiet would be able to kick his way to the surface and draw breath again. And in the midst of fighting, Nayeli recognized a lullaby that had granted her passage into so many childhood dreams.

She looked over her shoulder at the weeping spirit, and spoke her heart into the water as only her kind could: *I'm not alone anymore. I'm not lost, and you don't have to worry. I can claim the skin as mine once more, but you have to let me. You have to let go one more time, or I will truly be lost.*

Please, don't take this love from me, too.

The skin came away from Chris, then, and those slits in Nayeli's own palms opened to receive the anchors that would bind it to her once more. He was unconscious and couldn't make it to the surface himself, but that didn't matter, because this second skin was hers again, and slick as a seal, she pulled him up and got his head above water, then dragged him to the banks of the river and pressed on his chest and blew breath down his throat until his breath was his own again.

He blinked his eyes open. "Nayeli?"

She smiled down at him. "I told you that you'd gotten it wrong."

Then she lifted her head to look out at the water, seeking the form of a woman who'd loved her so much she'd given her skin and her life, in turn. But there was no trace of a figure to be found anywhere above the water, which rolled along gently under the early light of dawn as though it had never taken a soul into its depths.

Acknowledgments

This is an odd little collection that came together during a very difficult year. Nevertheless, it is dear to me, and it would not have come to fruition without the help of some very special people.

Gratitude first and foremost to my writing critique partners, Sara Carrero and Eva Papka, whose wisdom informed every page and whose loving shouts of encouragement are the best weapon I have against self-doubt. Thank you both for believing in this one. To further demonstrate my gratitude and to make up for our lost year of writing retreat, I *might* follow you into nature again on the next one (no promises, though).

For their consistent support, I am grateful to my lovely family of friends. Special thanks to those of you who've expressed excitement for this collection, those who've answered the phone to let me wail about writing it, and those who are always there to cheer me on in my writing endeavors, including: Jonathan Alexandratos, Fernanda de Ávila, Tracy Bealer, Brianna Beard, Maureen Boles, Cesar Bustamante, Carmen Cabello, Catherine Carl, Kelly Centrelli, Courtney Cloud, Jenny Cordella, Alexis Daria, Barbara Emanuele, Grant Faulkner, Alexis Garay, Yanina Goldstein, Heather M. Gooden, Ginalysse Ingles, Christina Jen, Shifa Kapadwala, Camille Lofters, Jessica Lynn, Robert Palmer, Megan Pindling, Rich Pisciotta, Shanika Powell, Michelle Reynoso, John Rice,

Martha Roldan, Emily Rosewood, Lisa Schell, Kate Schnur, Jamison Standridge, John Troynaski, Rebecca Villarreal, Erik Wade, Emily Wasserman, Omari Weekes.

To my friends in library world who've helped me attain and manage my day jobs in the stacks all while typing away at this manuscript in the midst of a pandemic, thank you for being incredible literacy advocates, badass colleagues, and just generally inspiring people despite the most bizarre professional year I hope we ever have to experience! I'm especially thinking of: Rachel Altvater, Judy Axler, Stephanie Drucker, Kristina Fuessler, James Grzybowski, Sabrina Krug, Olivia Laurendi, Nathalie Levin, Marissa Lieberman, Jackie Lopez, Jen Marino, Jen Marroquin, Michelle Minervini, Daniella Pagán, Sabine Pierre, Jen Rebmann, Jean Rheingold, Michele Rudzewick, Jane Sullivan, Amanda Tucci. This was a tough year for authors and readers alike; thanks to efforts like yours, it was much better than it might have been.

To my parents: thank you for accepting that you have a child strange enough to pen this collection. I'm glad that all of the murder made you chuckle, Dad. Mom, I can't promise that no one's going to die in the next one, and I hope you'll forgive me for killing off so many characters (again). Endless love to both of you, of course, despite my murderous ways.

Danny, we made it through this absolute clusterfuck of a year together, and for that I am grateful beyond words. I love you, always, and I'm so proud of you. Let's never do another year like this again, okay?

Melissa Bobe is the author of the fantasy novel *Nascent Witch* and the weird fiction novella *Sibyls*. Her story "Necromancy" appears in the steampunk fairytale anthology *Clockwork, Curses, and Coal*, and she has more short fiction on the way. A recovering academic, she now works as a librarian. When she's not writing, Melissa spends her time spoiling her four rescue cats, cooking up new recipes for the people she loves, obsessing over ballet and beekeeping, and testing the limits of caffeine consumption.

Made in the USA
Middletown, DE
23 June 2025